THE UNTOLD SECRETS

THE ENIGMATIC AND ADVENTURE CHRONICLES

CHIYA ILLINOIS

Made with ♥ on the Notion Press Platform
www.notionpress.com

In the tapestry of tales woven within these pages, I dedicate this collection to the three pillars of my world. You are the constants in the ever-shifting narratives of my life, and it is with immense gratitude and love that I acknowledge your roles in the creation of this diverse mosaic of stories. Their belief in my passion has been the guiding force behind the creation of this novel.

To Nitin Agarwal, my literary mentor and guide, your passion for storytelling has been the compass that steered me through the intricate plots and twists of each narrative. Your love for the written word echoes in every tale, a testament to the inspiration drawn from your own narratives.

To Konpal Pareek, the muse whose unwavering support and boundless love have fueled my imagination. Your nurturing spirit has been the fertile soil in which the seeds of creativity have blossomed into the myriad stories that now find a home in this collection.

To Shivansh Agarwal, my companion in adventure and mischief, your lively spirit injects each story with the excitement of exploration and the delight of shared escapades. I write these stories solely because of your constant desire to hear them, which often compels me to craft on-the-spot tales, in the end, inspiring various other story ideas. This dynamic has infused each narrative with additional layers of depth and enthusiasm, bringing them to life in a more vivid and vibrant manner.

To my readers, your embrace of my work and the worlds I weave fuels the fire of my imagination. Your appreciation is the heartbeat that resonates through every page. I extend my deepest appreciation to the readers who have followed my literary endeavors. Your continued support and enthusiasm inspire me to push the boundaries of my storytelling.

This novel, a product of my love for the English language and my dedication to the craft, is a journey into the realms of suspense, friendship, and the resilience of the human spirit. I hope to convey the enduring power of camaraderie in the face of adversity.

As I venture into the realms of mystery, thrills, horrors, and adventures, I carry with me the lessons of resilience, love, and camaraderie that you have imparted. This collection is not just a reflection of my imagination but a tribute to the tapestry of our shared experiences and the stories we continue to weave together.

This novel is not just a narrative; it is a testament to the passion that drives me, the encouragement that surrounds me, and the joy of creating stories that resonate with you, my cherished audience.

With love and gratitude,

Deetya Agarwal Pareek

Contents

Contents

Foreword

In the realm of storytelling, each tale is a whispered invitation to embark on a journey into uncharted territories of the imagination. As the author of this collection, I am both humbled and exhilarated to extend such an invitation to you, dear reader.

This compilation is more than just a gathering of narratives; it is a manifestation of a lifelong love with words and the inexhaustible magic they possess. To pen a foreword is to offer a glimpse into the essence of these stories, a preamble to the adventures awaiting you within the pages.

Within this bright collection of tales, you will find threads of suspense, friendship, and the unwaveing resilience of the human spirit. The characters embody facets of the human experience, and their journeys are intricately woven to explore the enduring power of companionship amidst the trials of life.

I owe a debt of gratitude to my parents, Nitin Agarwal and Konpal Pareek, whose unwavering support and belief in my passion for storytelling kindled the creative spark that has fueled this endeavor. To you, my cherished readers, your embrace of my previous works has been the guiding light that propels me to delve deeper into the realms of imagination.

As you embark on this literary odyssey, I invite you to lose yourself in the intricacies of each narrative, to feel the heartbeat of the characters, and to share in the joy of exploration. Your continued support is the compass that guides me, and for that, I am truly grateful.

May these words serve as companions, offering solace, excitement, and moments of reflection. It is my sincere hope that this collection resonates with you, transporting you to worlds both familiar and fantastical, leaving an indelible mark on your own tapestry of experiences.

Preface

Welcome, dear reader, to the threshold of a literary journey that we are about to embark upon together. As the author of this collection, I am delighted to share with you a glimpse behind the curtain, a prelude to the stories that await your discovery within these pages.

In crafting this anthology, I sought to create a tapestry of tales that reflects the diverse hues of the human experience—stories that resonate, challenge, and ultimately, transport us to realms both ordinary and extraordinary. Each narrative is a testament to the power of storytelling to weave connections across time and space.

The characters you will encounter are, in many ways, reflections of the multifaceted nature of humanity. Their struggles, triumphs, and the bonds they forge serve as a mirror to our own lives, inviting you to find echoes of your own journey within these fictional worlds.

I owe an immense debt of gratitude to my parents, Nitin Agarwal and Konpal Pareek, who nurtured my passion for storytelling from its nascent stages. Their unwavering support has been the bedrock upon which these tales have been built.

To you, my dear readers, I extend heartfelt thanks for your continued encouragement and enthusiasm. Your willingness to embark on literary adventures with me is both an honor and a source of inspiration.

As we turn the page together, let the narratives unfold, and may the stories within this collection resonate with you, spark your imagination, and, above all, provide moments of escape and reflection.

Acknowledgements

Writing a collection of stories is a journey that involves the support and encouragement of numerous individuals who contribute to the tapestry of creativity. I extend my heartfelt gratitude to those whose presence has been instrumental in shaping this literary endeavor.

First and foremost, I express my deepest appreciation to my parents, Nitin Agarwal and Konpal Pareek, whose unwavering belief in my passion for storytelling has been the guiding force behind this collection. Your love and encouragement have been the bedrock upon which these stories stand.

I express heartfelt gratitude to my mentors, who consistently recognized the potential within me and offered invaluable insights, feedback, and support during my learning journey. Your wisdom and encouragement have enriched the narratives within these pages.

A special acknowledgment to my readers, whose enthusiasm for my previous works has fueled my creative spirit. Your engagement and appreciation are the driving force behind my commitment to crafting engaging and meaningful stories.

To my friends and family who stood by me during the highs and lows of this creative journey, your support has been both uplifting and inspiring. Thank you for being the pillars of strength that every storyteller needs.

Lastly, but certainly not least, I express my gratitude to the literary community and fellow authors who continue to inspire me with their work. Your contributions to the world of storytelling motivate me to push the boundaries of my own creativity.

This collection is a testament to the collective efforts of a supportive community, and I am fortunate to have such wonderful individuals in my life. Thank you for being a part of this journey.

With sincere appreciation,
Deetya Agarwal Pareek

Prologue

In the dimming twilight between reality and imagination, a door opens to the extraordinary. Within the confines of these pages, you are about to embark on a journey that transcends the ordinary and plunges into the realms of mystery, thrills, and the enigmatic.

The characters seen in the stories, whose destinies are intricately woven into the fabric of stories waiting to unfold. Each tale possesses character with different backstories that mirrors the intricate dance of light and shadow, where the ordinary conceals the extraordinary.

As we step into their worlds, be prepared for suspense that lingers in the air like a haunting melody, friendships that withstand the tests of time, and the unyielding resilience of the human spirit in the face of the unknown.

The stage is set, the curtain drawn. The stories within this collection are whispers from the universe, calling you to join the characters on their journey. For within the turning of each page lies the promise of discovery, the thrill of the unknown, and the magic of storytelling.

Let the mysterious adventures begin!

SKYBOUND RESILIENCE

A group of ninth-grade students eagerly set off for a school program scheduled in Delhi, gleaming with excitement and anticipation. However, their journey takes an unforseen turn as an unexpected occurrence casts doubt upon their arrival in the bustling city.

I

INCEPTION OF UNCERTAINITY

As the morning sun painted the sky in hues of orange and pink, casting a warm glow over the landscape, our tight-knit group of friends gathered at the airport with palpable excitement. It was the beginning of an adventure that held the promise of a lifetime. Among us were familiar faces that had shared countless memories and moments of laughter.

Shruti, my best friend since childhood, was there with her infectious enthusiasm, her eyes sparkling with anticipation. Ishaan, the adventurous soul always ready for the next challenge, exchanged knowing smiles with Divya, the quiet but observant friend whose presence added depth to our group dynamics. Naomi, with her artistic flair, already had a sketchbook in hand, ready to capture the beauty of our journey. Rishik, the joker of the pack, couldn't resist cracking a joke, setting the tone for the lightheartedness that would accompany us throughout. Prisha, the thoughtful and caring soul, made sure everyone felt included and comfortable. And overseeing our spirited group was our teacher, Mrs. Kapoor, a guiding presence who balanced authority with a genuine love for teaching and fostering our curiosity.

The air was charged with anticipation as we checked in and prepared for the school program in Delhi, a city brimming with history, culture, and the promise of new experiences. Our chatter filled the air, a symphony of laughter and shared excitement, as we embarked on this journey together, ready to create memories that would last a lifetime. The adventure had just begun, and the vibrant colors of the morning sky seemed to foreshadow the vibrancy that awaited us in the bustling streets of Delhi.

The excitement in the air was palpable as Mrs. kapoor and the school meticulously planned our much-anticipated trip to Delhi, a city steeped in history and cultural richness. They had spent weeks researching the myriad historical sites, vibrant markets, and eclectic neighborhoods, creating an itinerary that promised an immersive experience. The prospect of exploring Delhi's diverse tapestry of heritage, from ancient monuments to modern landmarks, fueled our anticipation.

As the departure date drew near, the anticipation reached new heights. We eagerly anticipated the blend of old and new that Delhi promised – from the ancient historical monuments like the Red Fort and Qutub Minar to the contemporary vibrancy of markets like Chandni Chowk and the trendy neighborhoods that dotted the city. Our diverse group, each with their unique personalities and energies, created a perfect blend of excitement, laughter, and shared experiences.

Mrs. Kapoor, moved among us with a reassuring smile. She had encouraged our excitement, recognizing the educational value of our trip. As we exchanged stories and shared our expectations for the journey, Mrs. Kapoor's presence added a sense of guidance and responsibility to our group.

The airport terminal was alive with our laughter and animated conversations. Backpacks slung over our shoulders, boarding passes in hand, we eagerly awaited our flight to Delhi. The promise of adventure hung in the air as we imagined the experiences that awaited us—historic landmarks, local delicacies, and the bonding that comes from shared adventures.

As we boarded the plane, the cabin resonated with our excitement. Little did any of us know that this seemingly routine journey was about to take an unexpected and dangerous turn. The cabin crew went about their tasks, and the plane taxied on the runway, ready to ascend into the vast sky.

I settled into my seat, glancing around at my friends, oblivious to the unforeseen challenges that lay ahead. The thrill of the adventure ahead, the companionship of our group, and Mrs. Kapoor's watchful eye filled the air. Little did I know that the normalcy of this departure would soon be shattered by events that would test our friendships and resilience in ways we could never have imagined.

II

THE UNEXPECTED TURN

The hum of conversation and the low rumble of the plane's engines provided a steady soundtrack as we settled into our seats, anticipation and excitement bubbling among the passengers. Mrs. Kapoor, a familiar face in the row ahead, exuded a calming presence that served as an anchor in the face of the unknown journey that lay ahead.

As the plane gracefully soared through the skies, exchanging excited glances with Shruti and the rest of our group became a shared expression of our collective anticipation. Little did we know that an unforeseen threat loomed on the horizon, ready to shatter the peacefulness of the journey.

Suddenly, the ambient hum of the cabin was disrupted as the lights flickered, casting an uncanny ambiance throughout. Confusion rippled through the passengers like a wave, and a hush descended as the realization of an impending danger settled over us like a heavy fog.

In a matter of seconds, the atmosphere shifted from one of excitement to dread. The cockpit door violently burst open, revealing a group of menacing figures armed with weapons. The sudden intrusion sent shockwaves through the cabin, and fear paralyzed us as the hijackers swiftly seized control of the aircraft. Mrs. Kapoor, normally composed and unflappable, now wore an expression of disbelief as she, too, became a hostage to the unfolding chaos.

The once-familiar surroundings of the airplane cabin transformed into an unsettling scene of uncertainty. The hijackers, their faces coverd by masks, moved with a calculated danger, barking orders that echoed against the backdrop of terrified whispers. Passengers clutched their seats, their eyes wide with fear, as the routine flight unexpectedly twisted into a nightmare.

The hijackers' motives remained unclear, leaving the cabin suspended in a surreal state of tension. The low hum of the plane's engines, once a source of comfort, now underscored the gravity of the situation. Each passing second felt like an eternity as we grappled with the realization that our journey had taken an unimaginable and risky turn.

As the hijackers maintained their control, Mrs. Kapoor's reassuring presence, now overshadowed by the grim circumstances, served as a stark reminder of the fragility of the moment. The plane, once a symbol of travel and adventure, had transformed into a confined space filled with uncertainty and fear.

The sudden turn of events had plunged the once joyous atmosphere into a chilling nightmare. The hijackers scanned the area, searching for potential hostages, and forcefully grabbed Shruthi and Divya by their hair, causing them to scream. Both the girls found themselves unexpectedly plunged into the heart of this dangerous situation, with their lives precariously hanging in the balance.

I was paralyzed by shock and horror, fixated on the plight of my friends Shruti and Divya. The use of human shields transformed the two unsuspecting girls into mere pawns in a perilous game of power and control. The gravity of the situation hit me like a sledgehammer, extinguishing the initial excitement that had accompanied the trip.

As panic swept through the cabin like wildfire, the passengers grappled with the harsh reality of their plight. The once-thriving friendship had given way to a palpable tension, leaving everyone on edge. The hijackers, with authority in their voices, issued commands that echoed ominously in the confined space, creating an atmosphere of fear and submission.

Amidst the chaos, Mrs. Kapoor, usually a source of reassurance, exchanged a meaningful glance with the students. Her eyes communicated a silent plea for composure and resilience in the face of adversity. It was a moment that demanded strength, as the passengers grappled with the surreal shift from a carefree journey to a life-threatening ordeal.

The thrill that had initially fueled the excitement for the trip now coursed through everyone's veins in a surge of fear and uncertainty.

In that fateful moment, the airplane ceased to be a vessel of adventure and exploration; instead, it morphed into an ominous stage for a harrowing drama. The lives of Shruti, Divya, and every soul on board hung precariously in the balance, their fate at the mercy of the hijackers orchestrating this dangerous plot.

The hijackers' ominous presence loomed over us, their authority cutting through the air like a chilling wind. The weight of their demands hung heavily in the cabin, each command intensifying the sense of vulnerability that gripped us all. It was a surreal and terrifying contrast to the carefree excitement that had initially fueled our journey.

Amidst this chaos, my mind raced with thoughts of our group of friends and the uncharted territory we now found ourselves navigating. The strength of our bonds, once forged in moments of joy and camaraderie, faced an unprecedented challenge. As fear and uncertainty tightened their grip, I wondered if our friendships would prove resilient enough to weather this impending storm.

I couldn't shake the nagging uncertainty about what lay ahead. In the face of this unexpected adversity, the airplane became a crucible for our friendships, testing whether the ties that bound us could endure the strain of a perilous journey none of us had anticipated.

III

THE CALM BEFORE THE STORM

Mrs. Kapoor, our teacher and a source of guidance, exchanged a solemn look with me, her eyes conveying an unspoken understanding. The once-confident authority figure was now a fellow passenger, equally caught in the web of uncertainty. The gravity of the situation settled over us like a heavy fog, making it clear that our journey had taken an unexpected and dangerous turn.

I turned to my friends, the familiar faces of Ishaan, Divya, Naomi, Rishik, and Prisha reflecting the same fear and determination that churned within me. It was a silent pact among us—we needed to remain united, to think strategically, and to find a way to overcome the looming threat.

The hijackers, oblivious to the subtle communication happening among our group, continued to assert their control. The atmosphere inside the plane was thick with fear, the muffled sounds of sobbing and hushed conversations creating a dissonant backdrop to the high-stakes drama playing out before us.

In that moment, I felt a surge of determination. My focus sharpened on the details—the number of hijackers, their movements, any signs of vulnerability. The plane continued its course, hurtling through the sky as I mentally mapped out potential escape routes and strategies to outsmart those who held us captive.

As the minutes passed, my role within the group became clear. I needed to be the eyes and ears, the one who would observe, analyze, and, when the time was right, act decisively. Little did I know that this unwelcome role would thrust me into the forefront of our group's fight for survival—a fight that held the promise of not only freeing Shruti and Divya but ensuring the safety of every soul on that plane.

As the observer and strategist in this harrowing situation, my senses heightened, attuned to every shade that unfolded within the confined space of the aircraft. The dire reality of the circumstance gripped my awareness, a palpable tension hanging thick in the air. The hijackers, masters of cold and methodical actions, had deftly separated Shruti and Divya from the rest of us, their calculated moves casting a chilling shadow of fear over the entire cabin.

In the midst of this unfolding nightmare, my eyes instinctively sought out Shruti, and in that shared gaze, a silent communication passed between us. It was an unspoken acknowledgment of the shared distress that had seamlessly woven itself into the fabric of our reality. The once-familiar confines of the airplane now seemed alien and threatening, the ambient hum of engines transformed into a disconcerting soundtrack to our collective unease.

The cabin was filled with a profound and echoing silence. Shruti and Divya, symbols of our collective vulnerability, were now physically bound, their freedom stripped away by the unyielding constraints of the cold, metallic restraints. Helplessness enveloped me, a suffocating cloak that tightened with each passing moment.

As the hijackers led Shruti and Divya away, the determination etched in Shruti's eyes became a beacon of strength that cut through the darkness. It was a silent promise, a flame of resilience that refused to be extinguished. In that moment, her unwavering resolve became a source of inspiration, fueling my own determination to navigate this ordeal with strategic acumen.

In the face of adversity, the role of the observer and strategist took on a newfound significance, each decision weighed with the gravity of the situation. As we hurtled through the skies, the confines of the airplane became a crucible, testing the limits of our strength, resilience, and the bonds that held us together in the face of the unknown.

The hijackers, concealed behind masks that rendered their expressions unreadable, continued to wield control with an unsettling air of unpredictability. My mind raced, navigating a mental labyrinth of urgency as it grappled with the pressing need to act within the confinements of limited options. Each passing minute felt like an lengthy hour, the gravity of the situation hanging heavy in the air. I strained to eavesdrop on their conversations, desperately hoping to know even the slightest snippet of information that could become a crucial puzzle piece in formulating a plan for escape.

Meanwhile, amidst the rest of the group, our silent communication emerged as a lifeline of its own. Glances exchanged between us conveyed volumes, a tacit understanding that strengthened our collective resolve to endure and overcome. In the unspoken language that unfolded in those shared looks, there existed a commitment to remain steadfast and find a way out of this nightmarish scenario. The weight of responsibility bore down on me, a heavy burden accentuated by the realization that the safety of Shruti, Divya, and the entire group rested on our collective ability to outsmart our captors.

As the drama continued to unfold, I couldn't help but wonder about Shruti's thoughts. Her resilience, palpable in the air, reverberated through the confined space. I envisioned the silent conversations she might be having with Divya, a nuanced exchange of unspoken reassurances that only true friendship could provide in times of crisis. In the crucible of this dire situation, the bond that held our group together faced its most severe test. It was a test not only of our ability to navigate the perilous circumstances but also a trial of the strength of our interpersonal connections and shared determination to emerge from this ordeal unbroken.

In the dimly lit cabin, the air hung heavy with tension, a palpable manifestation of the adversity that gripped us. The atmosphere was charged, and every creak of the aging floorboards seemed to echo the uncertainty that loomed over our small group. Shruti, with her hands bound and a defiant glint in her eyes, became the unexpected source of strength that fueled my determination.

As an observer thrust into a role of unexpected responsibility, I found myself deciphering the cryptic puzzle laid out before us. The events leading to Shruti's captivity were shrouded in mystery, and the weight of the unknown pressed on me as I pieced together the fragments of information available. The gravity of the situation hung in the air, demanding swift and calculated action.

Shruti's eyes, however, spoke volumes. They were windows to a resilience that refused to be broken by the adversity that had befallen her. In the face of the unknown fate she faced, her determination resonated like a silent call to arms. It was a stark reminder that, despite the dire circumstances, strength could be drawn from the unyielding spirit within.

Our roles, once aligned in pursuit of a shared journey, had diverged sharply. Shruti and Divya, the captives, embodied the struggles we faced, while I, the observer-turned-strategist, shouldered the responsibility of weaving a plan from the threads of uncertainty. The cramped cabin became a crucible where destinies were forged, and the unfolding events threatened not only to reshape our journey but also redefine the very essence of the friendships that bound us.

Little did I expect that the confined space in that cabin would become the crucible for a transformation that extended beyond the physical boundaries of our immediate predicament. The friendships we once took for granted were now tested by the crucible of adversity. Each decision, each revelation, added a layer of complexity to the intricate tapestry of our relationships.

In the face of uncertainty, our collective resilience emerged as the guiding force. The uncertain path that lay ahead demanded a level of fortitude we hadn't known we possessed. As the events unfolded, we found ourselves navigating not only the physical challenges of our journey but also the intricate dynamics of camaraderie, trust, and the unspoken bonds that held us together.

In the end, the determination in Shruti's eyes became the beacon that guided us through the storm. The cramped cabin became a symbol of transformation, where adversity tested the limits of our strength and unity. As we ventured into the uncertain path ahead, the echoes of that pivotal moment lingered, shaping not just our journey but also the very core of who we were to become.

IV

THE RISING STORM

With Shruti and Divya taken hostage, the rest of us—Ishaan, Naomi, Rishik, Prisha, and Mrs. Kapoor—huddled together, our eyes reflecting a mixture of fear and determination. The hijackers, temporarily focused on their own activities, provided a brief window for us to regroup and assess our situation.

Ishaan, ever level-headed, took charge, suggesting that we pool our resources and intellect to navigate this perilous situation. Mrs. Kapoor, retained a sense of composure that spoke to her years of experience in guiding students through challenging circumstances. We formed a makeshift alliance, recognizing the urgent need for coordination.

Naomi's knowledge of Morse code emerged as an unexpected but valuable asset. We had all learnt a bit of the language from her, and it turned out to be valuable. The idea of using Morse code to communicate discreetly gained unanimous approval. The rhythmic tapping of fingers against the armrests became our clandestine language, allowing us to share information without alerting the hijackers to our efforts.

In those moments, our unity became our greatest strength. Each member of our group brought a unique skill set to the table. Ishaan's leadership, Naomi's ingenuity with Morse code, Rishik's resilience, Prisha's unwavering spirit, and Mrs. Kapoor's guidance formed a cohesive force. Together, we plotted and planned, aiming to outsmart the hijackers and ensure the safety of everyone on board.

As the tension within the cabin escalated, Naomi's expertise in Morse code became a lifeline for our group. The rhythmic tapping of fingers against the armrests transformed the confines of the plane into a clandestine communication hub.

Naomi's coded messages conveyed critical information without the hijackers suspecting a thing. Updates on their movements, potential escape routes, and words of encouragement passed between us in the silent language of dots and dashes. The cabin, once steeped in fear, now echoed with the rhythmic language of hope.

Naomi's role transcended her initial expertise; she became the orchestrator of our silent symphony. Each tap, each pause, carried the weight of our collective determination to resist the hijackers and ensure the safety of everyone on board. The Morse code, initially a method of communication, became a metaphor for our group's resilience.

As we hurtled through the sky, the coded messages served as a silent promise—a promise that we would face the unknown together, armed with the strength of unity and the indomitable spirit to defy the odds. Naomi's ingenuity, coupled with the collective resolve of our group, turned the plane into a realm where hope persisted, even in the face of the darkest adversity.

As the rhythmic tapping of Morse code echoed through the cabin, a silent determination settled over our group. Rishik, known for his quick thinking and decisiveness, emerged as a natural leader in this crisis. His keen observations and analytical mind became instrumental in our collective effort to navigate the perilous situation.

Rishik took the initiative to survey the cabin discreetly, gathering crucial information about the hijackers‘ positions and activities. His ability to remain composed under pressure became a source of inspiration for the rest of us. With each coded message from Naomi, Rishik devised a plan, mapping out potential escape routes and identifying vulnerabilities in the hijackers' control. Then Rishik conveyed us a message that there were 5 men in total, to in the back, 2 in the cockpit and one who kept moving around the plane back and forth, according to Rishik, The man moving back and forth's gun wasnt loaded, so it would be an eary escape for us if we got that gun in our hand.

The rest of us, including Ishaan, Prisha, and Mrs. Kapoor, looked to Rishik for guidance. His calm demeanor and strategic approach reassured us, instilling a sense of confidence in our ability to overcome the seemingly insurmountable challenge. Then Rishik conveyed us a message that there were 5 men in total, to in the back, 2 in the cockpit and one who kept moving around the plane back and forth, according to Rishik, The man moving back and forth's gun wasnt loaded, so it would be an eary escape for us if we got that gun in our hand.

We continued to tap out Morse code messages.

The plane, once a vessel of routine travel, had become a stage for resilience and determination, with each member playing a crucial role in the unfolding drama. We awaited the opportune moment to put our plans into action.

The tension within the hijacked plane reached the peak as our group, led by Rishik's strategic initiatives, continued to exchange information through Morse code. The hijackers remained unaware of the silent symphony of communication taking place under their noses.

Rishik's observational skills and decisive actions became the linchpin of our response. He devised a plan that hinged on exploiting the hijackers‘ vulnerabilities, meticulously considering every detail to ensure the safety of Shruti, Divya, and the entire group.

Naomi's Morse code messages served as a lifeline, relaying updates on the hijackers' movements and actions. Each tap communicated a piece of the puzzle, allowing us to form a comprehensive understanding of the situation. As Rishik continued to orchestrate our collective efforts, a palpable sense of anticipation hung in the air.

Our group, bound by a shared commitment to overcome adversity, awaited the opportune moment to put Rishik's plan into action. As we tapped out our coded messages, we exchanged determined glances, silently affirming our readiness for whatever lay ahead.

The unfolding drama within the hijacked plane became a testament to the strength of friendship and the human spirit. Each member of our group played a vital role in this high-stakes narrative, and as the tension mounted, the collective hope for a successful resolution fueled our resilience. Little did we know that the climax of our struggle against the hijackers loomed on the horizon, promising a resolution that would define the outcome of our harrowing ordeal.

In the cabin, the hijackers' vigilance showed no signs of waning. Shruti and Divya, still held hostage, remained at the center of the ordeal. The rest of us, handcuffed and with our collective resolve intact, exchanged silent glances, our eyes conveying a shared understanding of the challenges that lay ahead.

Rishik, with his eyes constantly scanning the surroundings, signaled to us through subtle gestures. The coded messages had provided valuable insights into the hijackers' patterns, but the real test would be in translating that information into action.

Naomi, ever vigilant, continued to tap out Morse code messages, keeping us apprised of the hijackers' movements. The plan, meticulously crafted, relied on precision and unity. Each member of our group understood their role, and as the tension mounted, a quiet determination settled over us.

The hijackers, ensconced in their control of the plane, remained oblivious to the undercurrent of resistance brewing among the passengers. The cabin, once a confined space of fear, now held the promise of a silent uprising—a collective effort to reclaim control and ensure our safety.

As we neared the climax of our struggle, a sense of unity pervaded the group. The solidarity that had been forged through adversity became our greatest asset. The plane, suspended in the darkness of the night, carried the weight of our collective hopes and fears, each heartbeat echoing the silent countdown to the moment that would define the resolution of our harrowing ordeal.

Our group braced for the imminent challenge, knowing that the success of our plan would depend on swift and coordinated action. Little did we realize that the next chapter of our journey would be a test of courage, resilience, and the unyielding spirit of friendship that had carried us through the darkest hours of the hijacking.

V

THE UNFOLDING DRAMA

As the observer and strategist in this harrowing situation, my senses heightened, attuned to every shade that unfolded within the confined space of the aircraft. The dire reality of the circumstance gripped my awareness, a palpable tension hanging thick in the air. The hijackers, masters of cold and methodical actions, had deftly separated Shruti and Divya from the rest of us, their calculated moves casting a chilling shadow of fear over the entire cabin.

In the midst of this unfolding nightmare, my eyes instinctively sought out Shruti, and in that shared gaze, a silent communication passed between us. It was an unspoken acknowledgment of the shared distress that had seamlessly woven itself into the fabric of our reality. The once-familiar confines of the airplane now seemed alien and threatening, the ambient hum of engines transformed into a disconcerting soundtrack to our collective unease.

The cabin was filled with a profound and echoing silence. Shruti and Divya, symbols of our collective vulnerability, were now physically bound, their freedom stripped away by the unyielding constraints of the cold, metallic restraints. Helplessness enveloped me, a suffocating cloak that tightened with each passing moment.

As the hijackers led Shruti and Divya away, the determination etched in Shruti's eyes became a beacon of strength that cut through the darkness. It was a silent promise, a flame of resilience that refused to be extinguished. In that moment, her unwavering resolve became a source of inspiration, fueling my own determination to navigate this ordeal with strategic acumen.

In the face of adversity, the role of the observer and strategist took on a newfound significance, each decision weighed with the gravity of the situation. As we hurtled through the skies, the confines of the airplane became a crucible, testing the limits of our strength, resilience, and the bonds that held us together in the face of the unknown.

The hijackers, concealed behind masks that rendered their expressions unreadable, continued to wield control with an unsettling air of unpredictability. My mind raced, navigating a mental labyrinth of urgency as it grappled with the pressing need to act within the confinements of limited options. Each passing minute felt like an lengthy hour, the gravity of the situation hanging heavy in the air. I strained to eavesdrop on their conversations, desperately hoping to know even the slightest snippet of information that could become a crucial puzzle piece in formulating a plan for escape.

Meanwhile, amidst the rest of the group, our silent communication emerged as a lifeline of its own. Glances exchanged between us conveyed volumes, a tacit understanding that strengthened our collective resolve to endure and overcome. In the unspoken language that unfolded in those shared looks, there existed a commitment to remain steadfast and find a way out of this nightmarish scenario. The weight of responsibility bore down on me, a heavy burden accentuated by the realization that the safety of Shruti, Divya, and the entire group rested on our collective ability to outsmart our captors.

As the drama continued to unfold, I couldn't help but wonder about Shruti's thoughts. Her resilience, palpable in the air, reverberated through the confined space. I envisioned the silent conversations she might be having with Divya, a nuanced exchange of unspoken reassurances that only true friendship could provide in times of crisis. In the crucible of this dire situation, the bond that held our group together faced its most severe test. It was a test not only of our ability to navigate the perilous circumstances but also a trial of the strength of our interpersonal connections and shared determination to emerge from this ordeal unbroken.

In the dimly lit cabin, the air hung heavy with tension, a palpable manifestation of the adversity that gripped us. The atmosphere was charged, and every creak of the aging floorboards seemed to echo the uncertainty that loomed over our small group. Shruti, with her hands bound and a defiant glint in her eyes, became the unexpected source of strength that fueled my determination.

As an observer thrust into a role of unexpected responsibility, I found myself deciphering the cryptic puzzle laid out before us. The events leading to Shruti's captivity were shrouded in mystery, and the weight of the unknown pressed on me as I pieced together the fragments of information available. The gravity of the situation hung in the air, demanding swift and calculated action.

Shruti's eyes, however, spoke volumes. They were windows to a resilience that refused to be broken by the adversity that had befallen her. In the face of the unknown fate she faced, her determination resonated like a silent call to arms. It was a stark reminder that, despite the dire circumstances, strength could be drawn from the unyielding spirit within.

Our roles, once aligned in pursuit of a shared journey, had diverged sharply. Shruti and Divya, the captives, embodied the struggles we faced, while I, the observer-turned-strategist, shouldered the responsibility of weaving a plan from the threads of uncertainty. The cramped cabin became a crucible where destinies were forged, and the unfolding events threatened not only to reshape our journey but also redefine the very essence of the friendships that bound us.

Little did I expect that the confined space in that cabin would become the crucible for a transformation that extended beyond the physical boundaries of our immediate predicament. The friendships we once took for granted were now tested by the crucible of adversity. Each decision, each revelation, added a layer of complexity to the intricate tapestry of our relationships.

In the face of uncertainty, our collective resilience emerged as the guiding force. The uncertain path that lay ahead demanded a level of fortitude we hadn't known we possessed. As the events unfolded, we found ourselves navigating not only the physical challenges of our journey but also the intricate dynamics of camaraderie, trust, and the unspoken bonds that held us together.

In the end, the determination in Shruti's eyes became the beacon that guided us through the storm. The cramped cabin became a symbol of transformation, where adversity tested the limits of our strength and unity. As we ventured into the uncertain path ahead, the echoes of that pivotal moment lingered, shaping not just our journey but also the very core of who we were to become.

In the dimly lit cabin of the hijacked plane, the tension reached its max. Rishik's strategic planning and Naomi's Morse code messages had brought us to the brink of a decisive moment. As the plane continued its journey through the night, the weight of the impending climax pressed upon us like an inevitable storm.

Rishik, with a subtle nod, signaled the initiation of our plan—a plan that symbolized a collective stand against the oppression that had gripped us. The handcuffs, once symbols of helplessness, now became a metaphor for our shared commitment to break free from the hijackers' control. The atmosphere in the cabin crackled with an undercurrent of unity and determination.

Naomi's tapping fingers relayed the last-minute updates on the hijackers' positions in Morse code. The rhythmic language of dots and dashes became our silent communication, guiding our synchronized efforts. As the tension mounted, we exchanged glances that spoke volumes—a shared understanding that this was the moment we had been waiting for, the climax of our struggle.

The hijackers, still oblivious to the rising resistance, continued their vigilance over the cabin. Shruti and Divya, held captive, remained at the heart of our collective concern. The plan, crafted with meticulous precision, relied on seizing the element of surprise and disrupting the hijackers‘ control.

Rishik's leadership emerged as the linchpin of the decisive moment. The orchestrated chaos unfolded with a choreographed grace. Seated in the aisle, Ishaan extended his foot to trip the unarmed hijacker. In an instant, the remaining hijackers converged on the scene, leaving Divya and Shruthi and the cockpit unguarded. As they leaned down to assist the fallen hijacker, I and Ishaan swiftly confiscated their weapons from their belts, turning the tables on the hijackers. Meanwhile, Prisha and Mrs. Kapoor had abandoned their seats, rushing toward Divya and Shruthi, ushering them into the cockpit, As we diverted the hijackers' attention.

In the confined space of the plane, a micro-revolution erupted. Shouts of determination reverberated through the cabin, the scuffling of feet echoed against the walls, and the clash of wills became the anthem of our resistance.

As the uproar subsided, a collective exhale swept through the cabin. The miserable hijackers marked the end of our distressing ordeal. The plane, once a vessel of fear, had become the stage for a climactic triumph of resilience and unity—a testament to the indomitable spirit of those who had faced the storm together.

The culmination of our resistance left the hijacked plane in an eerie stillness. The hijackers, their authority dismantled by our collective defiance, sat defeated. We were limited in our capabilities, but we confidently demanded that all of them disarm, seizing control of their own weapons.

I glanced at my friends, our eyes telling stories of exhaustion and victory. Shruti and Divya, freed from their ordeal, embraced in a reunion, the tangible embodiment of the collective struggle we had faced.

Rishik, the architect of our resistance, surveyed the plane's interior. The signs of our struggle were etched in every scuff mark and overturned seat—a testament to the courage that had blossomed within each of us. Naomi, Ishaan, Prisha, and Mrs. Kapoor, all vital players in our collective defiance, shared a glance that conveyed the weight of our shared experience.

VI

LESSONS IN THE SKY

As the reality of our victory sank in, emotions swirled within me. The ordeal had tested the boundaries of our courage, but it had also woven bonds that transcended the ordinary. The victory wasn't just in reclaiming the plane; it was in discovering the resilience within ourselves and the strength that arose from our unity.

In the cockpit, the pilot relayed the news of our successful resolution to ground control. What had started as a threatening detour had transformed into a narrative of resilience and shared survival. The plane, having braved the storm, continued its journey with a renewed sense of purpose—a purpose rooted in the shared experience of overcoming adversity.

However, our triumph was accompanied by a reckoning. As the authorities took charge upon landing, questions loomed about the events leading to the hijacking. We found ourselves at the center of an investigation that would inspect the motives and mechanics behind the hijacking.

The journey, initially filled with the promise of a school program, had evolved into a saga of resilience and survival. Stepping off the plane, the collective gaze of our group shifted from the hijackers to the uncertain path that awaited us—a path where the emotional aftermath of our extraordinary journey would demand as much resilience as the physical ordeal we had just overcome.

In the days that followed the hijacking ordeal, our group grappled with the aftermath navigating both the investigation and the emotional aftermath of our shared experience. The skies, once the stage for a distressing drama, now held the echoes of a journey that had tested our limits and reshaped our perspectives.

The investigation shed light on the motives behind the hijacking, unraveling a complex web of circumstances. As we cooperated with authorities, the weight of our shared secret became a collective burden. The bond that had been forged in the crucible of adversity now faced the challenges of scrutiny and judgment.

All of us found comfort in each other's company, silent acknowledgments passing between us that transcended words. The friendships formed during that turbulent flight became a source of solace, a reminder that even in the face of chaos, connections could be forged that would withstand the test of time.

For me, the skies had become both a classroom and a canvas. Lessons of courage, unity, and resilience unfolded against the backdrop of the clouds. The plane, once a vessel of routine travel, had transformed into a realm where ordinary individuals had been thrust into an extraordinary narrative.

As we departed the airport, marking the end of our unexpected odyssey, the group dispersed, each carrying the weight of our shared journey into the world. The skies, having witnessed our triumph and the subsequent reckoning, continued to stretch endlessly above, indifferent to the human drama that had unfolded within their realm.

In the quiet moments that followed, I often found myself gazing at the sky, reflecting on the lessons learned and the bonds forged. The narrative, though marked by turbulence, had also revealed the strength that lay within ordinary individuals when faced with extraordinary circumstances.

And so, as the echoes of our journey lingered in the sky, the group moved forward, forever connected by an experience that had defied the ordinary and illuminated the resilience that resides within the human spirit. The plane, having weathered the storm, faded into the distance, leaving behind a story etched in the clouds—a story of survival, comaradeship , and the enduring impact of an unexpected journey in the skies.

HOTEL NOT FOUND

A group of office workers travels to New Zealand for a business trip, expecting routine affairs. However, their hotel unveils a dark past and secrets shrouded in mystery. As they uncover the enigma within its walls, the prospect of a safe return home becomes increasingly elusive.

VII

ARRIVAL

The flight to Queenstown unfolded without any notable incidents. The passengers, primarily composed of office workers, engaged in lively conversations, exchanging excitement about the impending business meetings and their plans to explore the picturesque landscapes of New Zealand. The collective anticipation of a routine yet invigorating affair in this beautiful country permeated the atmosphere.

As the plane descended over the Southern Alps, the passengers were treated to awe-inspiring views of snow-capped peaks and meandering rivers. The majestic scenery outside the aircraft windows set the stage for the adventure that awaited them on the ground.

Upon landing, the group was greeted by a refreshing mountain breeze, invigorating their senses as they disembarked from the aircraft. Moving towards a line of waiting cabs, they began their journey from the airport to Milford Manor, their designated accommodation for the trip.

The cab ride proved to be a visual feast as it navigated through the charming streets of Queenstown, often regarded as the "thriller capital of the world." The narrow streets unveiled a mix of quaint shops, bustling cafes, and captivating views of Lake Wakatipu. The passengers marveled at the vibrant atmosphere of the town, its unique blend of urban life with the surrounding natural beauty creating an enchanting experience.

As the cab wound its way through the town, the passengers glimpsed adventure enthusiasts preparing for various activities, such as bungee jumping, skydiving, and jet boating. The highly-fueled atmosphere added an extra layer of excitement to the already enchanting surroundings.

The journey to Milford Manor continued, with the cab traversing winding roads that offered panoramic views of the Southern Alps. The passengers couldn't help but be captivated by the sheer beauty of the landscapes unfolding before them. Snow-capped peaks, lush greenery, and pristine lakes contributed to the visual spectacle that defined Queenstown's allure.

As the cab approached Milford Manor, the excitement among the passengers reached its peak. They were eager to settle into their accommodations and begin their business endeavors, all while savoring the promise of exploration and adventure that Queenstown held for them during their stay.

The driver, with a hint of intrigue in his voice, shared a few narratives about the historic establishment. "It's a historic place," he remarked, his voice low and mysterious. "Some locals say it's got a history, but I reckon it's just stories to entertain the tourists."

The atmosphere inside the cab buzzed with a mix of curiosity and skepticism as the passengers listened to the driver's tales. However, their attention was soon diverted as the imposing the outline of Milford Manor emerged around a bend. The hotel stood proudly against the breathtaking backdrop of Lake Wakatipu and the towering mountains, instantly captivating the travelers with its old-world charm.

As the cab came to a halt at the grand entrance, the group couldn't help but marvel at the Victorian architecture that adorned Milford Manor. The intricate details and ornate features hinted at the hotel's rich history, adding to the air of mystery that the driver had alluded to. The well-manicured gardens surrounding the property further enhanced the elegant and timeless ambiance, creating a serene oasis against the stunning natural scenery.

The travelers exited the cab, their anticipation growing as they took in the grandeur of Milford Manor. The cool mountain breeze carried a sense of tranquility, contrasting with the whispered tales of the hotel's alleged history. With a mixture of excitement and intrigue, the group crossed the threshold, ready to embark on their stay at this enchanting retreat in the heart of Queenstown.

Upon entering the lobby, the atmosphere underwent a subtle transformation. The air seemed to grow still, and the soft flickering of candles on antique sconces cast dancing shadows on the walls. A palpable sense of nostalgia permeated the space, blending seamlessly with the distinct scents of aged wood and polished brass.

The group found themselves in the midst of an ambiance that evoked a bygone era, with each step resonating with the echoes of Milford Manor's storied past. The lobby's timeless decor and the play of shadows created an enchanting backdrop, leaving the travelers with a sense of awe and intrigue.

As they approached the reception desk, a poised woman, exuding an air of formality, greeted them warmly. "Welcome to Milford Manor. We trust you'll find your stay comfortable and enjoyable," she said with a practiced smile. However, her eyes betrayed a subtle hint of something unspoken, as if the hotel held secrets she dared not reveal. The momentary glint of mystery in her gaze only deepened the air of intrigue that hung in the lobby.

The receptionist efficiently handled the check-in process, providing each guest with keys to their rooms and offering information about the hotel's amenities. Despite the warmth in her voice, there was a quiet reserve, a suggestion that beneath the surface, Milford Manor harbored tales yet untold.

As the travelers made their way to their respective accommodations, the lobby's timeless charm lingered in their minds. The anticipation of exploring both the hotel's historic corridors and the captivating surroundings of Queenstown fueled a sense of excitement, mingled with the subtle allure of the mysteries hinted at by the receptionist's guarded demeanor.

The group received their room keys and made their way to their respective accommodations, passing through dimly lit hallways adorned with vintage tapestries and faded portraits. The creaking floorboards beneath their feet added to the eerie ambiance, though they dismissed it as the charm of an old building.

Little did they know that the routine business trip they expected was about to transform into a journey filled with mystery and the haunting secrets of Milford Manor. The hotel, with its timeless allure, seemed to pulse with an energy that transcended the ordinary. Each step they took echoed with the weight of history, and the shadows of the past, hidden within the nooks and crannies of the manor, patiently waited to reveal themselves to the unsuspecting visitors.

The group, armed with their room keys, ventured down dimly lit hallways adorned with vintage tapestries and faded portraits. The flickering glow of antique sconces cast fleeting shadows, and the creaking floorboards beneath their feet added an eerie quality to the ambiance. Some exchanged nervous glances, while others dismissed the unsettling sounds as mere quirks of charm in an old building.

As the group dispersed into their rooms, the air buzzed with a sense of anticipation. The travelers were yet to discover that beneath the veneer of routine, an enigmatic narrative was poised to unfold, drawing them into the captivating depths of Milford Manor and its intriguing history. The secrets of the past lingered, ready to cast their spell upon the unsuspecting guests, turning a seemingly ordinary business trip into a journey shrouded in mystery and the echoes of time.

VIII

THE UNSETTLING WELCOME

The office workers, a mix of excitement and fatigue coloring their expressions, settled into their respective rooms within Milford Manor. The deluxe grandeur of the hotel's exterior stood in stark contrast to the subtle unease that had settled among them since their arrival. The air within the hotel seemed charged with a mysterious energy, as if the very walls held secrets waiting to be discovered by those who dared to venture into its depths.

As the sun dipped below the mountains, casting shadows over the lake, darkness gradually enveloped Milford Manor. The group, feeling the pull of both curiosity and trepidation, reconvened in the lobby to discuss their plans for the evening. A subdued hush fell over the room, the flickering chandeliers casting a soft, ambient glow on the antique furnishings that adorned the space.

Whispers of speculation circulated among the office workers, their furtive glances reflecting a shared sense of intrigue. The hotel, with its historic charm and enigmatic atmosphere, had ignited a collective curiosity that surpassed the typical discussions of business agendas and travel itineraries. The promise of exploration now extended beyond the bounds of Queenstown's picturesque landscapes, reaching into the very heart of Milford Manor and its hidden secrets.

As the group deliberated their evening plans, the mysteries of the hotel seemed to linger in the air, adding an extra layer of anticipation to their already intriguing stay. Little did they know that the night held more than routine business discussions; it held the promise of unraveling the secrets concealed within the ancient walls of Milford Manor.

During dinner in the hotel's elegant dining room, the first signs of Milford Manor's mysterious nature began to manifest. The soft clinking of glasses and distant murmurs echoed through the hall, creating an eerie ambiance, especially since no other guests were visible. Some among the group claimed to catch fleeting glimpses of figures in period clothing, only to see them disappear around corners, leaving empty hallways upon investigation.

As the office workers finished their dinner and dispersed to explore the hotel, a sudden chill descended over the atmosphere. Whispers seemed to be carried on the breeze, as if the very walls were privy to conversations from a bygone era. The air itself felt charged with the weight of untold stories, stirring a sense of both fascination and unease among the group.

Within the library, a sanctuary adorned with antique books and plush furniture, an old, weathered manuscript detailing the history of Milford Manor beckoned to the curious. As one of the office workers leafed through its pages, the revelations within hinted at scandalous affairs, family disputes, and a tragic love story that unfolded within the walls of the manor. The secrets of Milford Manor, concealed for years, seemed to slowly reveal themselves, intertwining with the very fabric of the hotel's existence.

The group, now caught in a web of intrigue, exchanged knowing glances. The routine business trip had taken an unexpected turn into the realm of the enigmatic, as Milford Manor unveiled its hidden past, leaving the office workers with a blend of curiosity and apprehension about the mysteries that lay ahead.

Returning to their rooms, the group discovered that the unsettling aura persisted. A few among them reported hearing faint piano melodies drifting through the corridors, yet the source remained elusive. Sleep proved elusive as well, as dreams were punctuated by indistinct voices and shadows that seemed to move of their own accord.

The following morning, as the group gathered for breakfast in the hotel's sunlit conservatory, uneasy glances were exchanged. The events of the previous night lingered in their minds, creating an unspoken understanding among them. The routine business trip had taken an unexpected turn into the realm of the paranormal, and a collective decision seemed to form—an unspoken agreement to delve deeper into the mysteries surrounding Milford Manor.

Amidst the clinking of cutlery and the soft murmur of conversation, the office workers contemplated their next steps. The sunlit conservatory, though bathed in light, couldn't dispel the shadows of uncertainty that hung over the group. It was as if Milford Manor itself beckoned them to uncover its secrets, inviting them to explore the hidden corridors and unravel the enigma that had gripped the hotel since their arrival.

The day ahead held the promise of discovery, but also the weight of the unknown. As the group prepared to embark on their investigation, the air in the conservatory seemed to hum with anticipation, setting the stage for a journey that transcended the boundaries of their initial business agenda and thrust them into the heart of Milford Manor's mysterious past.

Approaching the hotel staff discreetly, the office workers inquired about the strange occurrences that had unsettled their stay. The responses they received were guarded, with staff members offering tight-lipped smiles and assuring them that such things were common in a place with so much history. It was as if a collective decision had been made to keep the secrets of Milford Manor veiled, leaving the office workers with more questions than answers.

Undeterred by the elusive replies, the group decided to take matters into their own hands and explore the hotel's nooks and crannies. The promise of discovery and unraveling the truth behind the unsettling welcome fueled their determination. Little did they know that their quest for answers would lead them deeper into the enigma of Milford Manor, where the past and present intertwined in a dance of secrets waiting to be revealed.

As the office workers ventured into the dimly lit corridors and hidden corners of the hotel, a sense of anticipation and trepidation hung in the air. Whispers of forgotten tales seemed to follow them, echoing through the hallways as they delved deeper into the heart of Milford Manor. Each door they opened, each staircase they climbed, unveiled more layers of the mysterious history that permeated the very essence of the hotel.

The group's exploration became a journey through time, where the boundaries between past and present blurred. Every discovery seemed to raise new questions, and the shadows that clung to the walls held fragments of stories yet untold. The enigma of Milford Manor unfolded like a complex puzzle, enticing the office workers to piece together the fragments and reveal the haunting truths that lay beneath the surface.

IX

UNVEILING THE MYSTERY

Determined to unravel the mysteries surrounding Milford Manor, the group embarked on a collective investigation, armed with curiosity and a growing sense of trepidation. They navigated the labyrinthine corridors and explored hidden corners of the historic hotel, determined to peel back the layers of its enigmatic past.

Their first significant breakthrough occurred in the form of a dusty library tucked away on the third floor. Rows of leather-bound books lined the shelves, and as the group sifted through the pages, they discovered an old journal belonging to Amelia Carter, the matriarch of the Carter family. The entries chronicled a tumultuous family history, revealing forbidden love, bitter rivalries, and a tragic series of events that had unfolded within the walls of Milford Manor.

Amelia's words painted a vivid picture of the past, describing the intricacies of her relationships with family members, the whispered scandals that had plagued the Carter name, and the haunting secrets that had become intertwined with the very essence of the hotel. The group was captivated by the unfolding narrative, each entry adding new layers to the multifaceted story of Milford Manor.

As they delved deeper into the journal, the atmosphere in the library seemed to thicken with the weight of the revelations. The echoes of Amelia's words resonated through the room, and the group realized that they were on the verge of uncovering the long-buried truths that had cast a shadow over the hotel for generations. The mystery of Milford Manor was slowly unraveling, and the group braced themselves for the profound impact that the revelations might have on both the present and the echoes of the past that lingered within the historic walls.

As the group pieced together the narrative from Amelia Carter's journal, they uncovered a forbidden love affair that had been at the heart of the mysteries surrounding Milford Manor. The clandestine romance had blossomed between Amelia's daughter, Isabella, and a mysterious artist named Samuel Whitman. Their love had been vehemently opposed by Isabella's brother, Edmund, igniting a family feud that tore at the fabric of the Carter household.

The journal revealed details of secret passages within the hotel that Isabella and Samuel had used for their stealthy rendezvous, adding a layer of intrigue to the unfolding tale. The group, now armed with this newfound knowledge, was determined to unearth the truth. They delved deeper into the hidden corners of Milford Manor, guided by the journal's clues.

As they explored, the group discovered concealed doorways and forgotten staircases that led to secret chambers filled with artifacts from the past. The air within these hidden spaces seemed to thicken with the weight of history, and each discovery brought them closer to unraveling the intricate web of secrets that had remained shrouded in darkness for generations.

The echoes of Isabella and Samuel's forbidden love affair reverberated through the hidden chambers, and the group sensed they were on the brink of a profound revelation. The artifacts spoke of a time long ago, preserving the emotions and struggles of those who had once inhabited the hotel. With each step, the office workers moved deeper into the heart of Milford Manor's past, determined to shed light on the forbidden love that had become a haunting specter within the historic walls.

As the group delved deeper into the hidden chambers and forgotten corners of Milford Manor, they found themselves entangled in the intricate web of relationships and betrayals that had defined the Carter family's existence. Each room seemed to whisper tales of love and heartbreak, as if the very walls retained memories of the past, carrying the weight of the emotions that had once played out within the historic confines.

Amelia's journal continued to be their guide, revealing that the Carter family had faced financial ruin, and the hotel, once a symbol of opulence, had become a place of desperation and sorrow. The entries chronicled a downward spiral, with each word painting a picture of the family's struggle to maintain the grandeur of Milford Manor amid mounting challenges.

The final entries in Amelia's journal detailed a tragic night when the family faced an irreversible loss, leaving behind a lingering sorrow that echoed through the ages. The group felt the weight of that sorrow as they moved through the hotel, and the air seemed heavy with the collective grief that had seeped into the very foundation of Milford Manor.

The revelations of the journal added a poignant layer to the already complex narrative, and the group found themselves grappling with the profound emotions that emanated from the shadows of the past. As they continued their exploration, the once-majestic hotel transformed before their eyes, revealing not just a place of beauty and elegance, but a witness to the profound struggles and heartaches that had unfolded within its walls. The office workers, now intimately connected with the Carter family's tragic tale, pressed on, driven by a deepening sense of responsibility to uncover the complete story that had been concealed for so long.

The group's investigation into Milford Manor took an unexpected and intensely personal turn as they found themselves connecting with the ghosts of the Carter family. Apparitions of the long-departed family members began to materialize, reenacting scenes from their troubled history. The travelers, once mere observers, now found themselves empathizing with the spectral figures, trapped in a timeless loop of unresolved conflicts.

As the layers of the mystery peeled away, the group faced a pivotal choice – to continue their quest for the truth, risking their own entanglement in the haunted history of Milford Manor, or to retreat and leave the past to rest in peace. The spectral reenactments evoked deep emotions, and the travelers were torn between the desire to unveil the complete narrative and the realization that meddling with the past might carry unforeseen consequences.

Driven by a sense of duty to bring closure to the long-buried stories, they pressed forward into the heart of

Milford Manor, determined to unravel the remaining secrets and uncover the truth that had eluded discovery for so long.

The air in the hotel seemed charged with a mix of anticipation and apprehension as the travelers delved deeper into the haunted history. The decision to face the ghosts head-on marked a point of no return, and the group steeled themselves for the profound revelations that awaited them within the historic walls of Milford Manor. The past and present intertwined, and the travelers embarked on a journey that transcended the boundaries of time, bound by an unspoken commitment to unveil the complete story and bring peace to the troubled spirits that lingered within the echoes of the past.

X

THE GHOST OF MILLFORD MANOR

The veil between the present and the past continued to thin as the office workers pressed on with their exploration of Milford Manor. Whispers of bygone conversations echoed through the hallways, and ghostly apparitions became a common sight, as if the spirits of the Carter family sought to communicate their untold stories to the living.

One evening, as the group gathered in the dimly lit parlor, a haunting piano melody began to fill the air. Entranced by the ethereal music, the office workers followed the melancholic notes to a forgotten ballroom hidden behind a tapestry-covered wall. There, in the soft glow of spectral light, the ghostly figure of Isabella Carter danced alone. Her ethereal gown swirled around her as she moved to the haunting tune, creating a poignant and mesmerizing scene that left the office workers both captivated and unnerved.

The room seemed frozen in time, the echoes of Isabella's dance transcending the boundaries between the past and the present. The office workers, mere observers in this ghostly spectacle, felt a deep connection to the tragedy that had unfolded within the walls of Milford Manor. Isabella's spectral presence conveyed a sense of longing and sorrow, and the air was thick with emotions that transcended the passage of time.

As the piano melody faded into the echoes of the night, the office workers remained in the ballroom, their minds grappling with the profound encounter. The line between reality and the supernatural had blurred, and the group found themselves drawn further into the intricate tapestry of Milford Manor's haunted history. The decision to confront the ghosts of the past had opened a door to a realm where the living and the spectral coexisted, leaving the office workers to navigate the haunting mysteries that awaited them in the dimly lit corridors and forgotten chambers of the historic hotel.

The apparitions within Milford Manor extended beyond the solitary figure of Isabella, as the group encountered the stern visage of Edmund Carter in the library. There, he seemed engaged in a heated argument with unseen adversaries, his spectral presence reenacting the intense conflicts that had once defined the Carter family. The tragedy of their history played out before the travelers' eyes, deepening the connection to the spirits that lingered within the historic hotel.

As the group became more entwined with the spectral drama, tensions among them began to rise. The emotional weight of the past, coupled with the intense personal experiences of encountering the ghostly apparitions, took a toll on their collective psyche. The once-cohesive team found themselves grappling with conflicting emotions and perspectives, their individual reactions to the supernatural manifestations causing strains within the group.

The lines between the living and the dead blurred with each encounter, and the distinction between reality and the supernatural became increasingly difficult to discern. The haunting echoes of the Carter family's tragedy seemed to reverberate not only through the historic walls but also within the dynamics of the office workers who had become unwitting participants in the spectral drama.

As the group navigated the thinning veil between the present and the past, they faced a dilemma. The allure of uncovering the complete story within Milford Manor was tempered by the growing tensions among them. The haunting mysteries that had drawn them in now posed a challenge – to confront not only the ghosts of the Carter family but also the internal conflicts that threatened to fracture the cohesion of the once-united team. The journey into the enigmatic depths of Milford Manor had taken an unforeseen turn, weaving together the supernatural and the interpersonal, leaving the office workers to grapple with the consequences of their pursuit of the haunted history that had long been concealed within the hotel's historic embrace.

In their relentless quest to uncover the truth, the office workers stumbled upon a forgotten séance room hidden in the depths of Milford Manor. The room's walls were adorned with symbols and sigils, suggesting that attempts had been made in the past to communicate with the otherworldly entities that haunted the historic hotel. As they delved into the room's history, a realization dawned upon the group – the spirits were bound by unresolved conflicts, and their liberation was key to breaking the curse that held Milford Manor in its spectral grip.

Faced with this revelation, the group confronted a pivotal decision: whether to confront the ghosts and aid them in finding closure or to flee from the haunted embrace of Milford Manor. As they gathered in the séance room, a collective sense of determination settled over them. Guided by the revelations found in Amelia's journal and their personal encounters with the spectral figures, the office workers embarked on a series of rituals aimed at unraveling the ties that bound the Pembroke family to the hotel.

The séance room, with its ancient symbols and lingering energy, became the focal point of their efforts. The group, united by a shared purpose, ventured into the unknown, utilizing their newfound knowledge to communicate with the spirits that roamed the historic corridors. Each ritual carried them deeper into the heart of Milford Manor's haunted history, testing their resolve and challenging the boundaries between the living and the dead.

As the séances unfolded, the group felt a profound connection to the spirits that had long been trapped within the hotel's spectral realm. The echoes of the past resonated through the séance room, and the office workers found themselves becoming conduits for the untold stories of the Carter family. The outcome of their efforts remained uncertain, but the group pressed forward, determined to break the curse that had bound Milford Manor in the shackles of its haunted history. The séance room became a crucible of both fear and hope, where the living and the dead converged in a shared quest for resolution and release.

The séance room transformed into a nexus of supernatural energy, and the group braced themselves for the unknown. The ghosts, sensing an opportunity for redemption, manifested more vividly, their ethereal forms expressing a mix of anguish and longing that seemed to transcend the boundaries of time.As the ritual unfolded, the air crackled with an otherworldly energy, and the boundaries between the living and the dead trembled. The office workers stood at the crossroads of the paranormal, their senses heightened as they sought to free Milford Manor from the shackles of its haunted past.

The spirits of the Carter family, bound by unresolved conflicts and lingering sorrows, reached out to the living. Their spectral forms moved through the séance room, and the air seemed to shimmer with the intensity of their emotions. The group, committed to aiding the spirits in finding closure, felt a profound connection with the otherworldly entities that hovered in the ethereal space.

The séance became a dance between the living and the dead, a delicate interplay of energies seeking resolution. The office workers, guided by the rituals and their shared determination, remained on the precipice of the unknown, uncertain of what awaited them as they ventured further into the realm of the paranormal.

As the séance reached its zenith, the office workers braced for the potential consequences of their actions. The haunted history of Milford Manor hung in the balance, and the group stood poised at the threshold of a transformative moment that would either free the hotel from its spectral grip or plunge them further into the depths of the supernatural mysteries that permeated its historic halls. The séance room, now a conduit between worlds, held the key to unlocking the secrets that had bound the Carter family and Milford Manor in a timeless dance of tragedy and redemption.

XI

THE FINAL REVELAITON

The séance room pulsed with an otherworldly energy as the office workers delved deeper into their ritual. The ghostly figures of the Carter family manifested with increasing clarity, their ethereal forms now desperate for release from the timeless limbo that bound them to Milford Manor.

The group, guided by the revelations from Amelia's journal, spoke words of understanding and compassion to the spirits. As they shared in the pain and sorrow of the Carter family's tragic history, the spectral figures began to respond, their haunting visages softening with a mix of relief and gratitude.

In the midst of the séance, the group discovered a hidden compartment within the room containing artifacts that held significant meaning to the Carter family. Among these items was a locket belonging to Isabella, a letter written by Samuel, and a faded portrait capturing a moment of fleeting happiness in the family's turbulent past.

As each artifact was uncovered, the emotional weight of the séance intensified. The air resonated with the echoes of a love lost, a family torn asunder, and the desperation that had driven the Carter family to their tragic fate. The group, now fully immersed in the spectral drama, felt a profound connection to the ghosts they sought to liberate.

With each heartfelt revelation, the atmosphere within Milford Manor began to shift. The once oppressive energy lifted, and the ghostly apparitions gradually faded away, leaving behind a palpable sense of resolution. The séance room, once a focal point for paranormal activity, grew tranquil as the echoes of the past settled into a quiet peace.

The office workers, exhausted yet triumphant, emerged from the séance room to find Milford Manor transformed. The once dimly lit corridors now bathed in warm light, and the air felt lighter, devoid of the lingering melancholy that had haunted the hotel. The group shared a collective sigh of relief, their eyes meeting with a newfound understanding of the weight they had lifted from Milford Manor.

As the night gave way to dawn, the travelers gathered once more in the lobby, their reflections mirroring the soft light that spilled through the windows. The once-haunted hotel now stood as a testament to the resilience of both the living and the dead, a place where the shadows of the past had been laid to rest.

The group, forever changed by their encounter with the paranormal, prepared to leave Milford Manor behind. The enigma that had gripped the hotel had been unraveled, and the business trip that began with routine affairs had become an unforgettable journey into the heart of New Zealand's haunted history.

With the first rays of sunlight casting a warm glow over Lake Wakatipu, the office workers departed from Milford

Manor, their memories filled with the echoes of a bygone era. The secrets and mysteries that had unfolded within the hotel's walls were now mere whispers on the breeze, as they set out on their journey home, carrying with them the profound lessons learned from the enigmatic Milford Manor.

The morning sun bathed Milford Manor in a golden glow as the office workers prepared to depart from the now-transformed hotel. The weight of the supernatural encounter lingered, but a sense of closure and resolution accompanied them as they gathered their belongings and made their way to the lobby.

The once-stern receptionist, her demeanor softened, bid them farewell with a knowing smile. It seemed as though the entire hotel staff had sensed the shift in energy, acknowledging the subtle transformation that had taken place within Milford Manor.

As the group stepped out into the crisp New Zealand morning, a collective sigh of relief escaped their lips. The air was fresh, and the breathtaking scenery that had been overshadowed by the hotel's haunted history now revealed itself in all its splendor.

They glanced back at Milford Manor, its Victorian facade standing tall against the backdrop of Lake Wakatipu. The ghosts of the Carter family, now at peace, were nowhere to be seen. The once-darkened windows glowed with the promise of a new day.

The journey back to the airport was filled with a reflective silence. Each member of the group carried the weight of the paranormal encounter, a shared experience that had forged a bond among them. Their perspectives on the routine business trip had been forever altered, and the memories of Milford Manor lingered in the recesses of their minds.

During the flight home, conversations revolved around the events that had unfolded within the haunted hotel. The travelers shared their reflections on the impact of the supernatural encounter, pondering the thin line between the living and the dead and the profound effect it had on their own perceptions of reality.

As the plane touched down in their home country, the office workers dispersed, each carrying the memories of Milford Manor in their hearts. The routine business trip had become an extraordinary journey into the unknown, revealing the resilience of the human spirit and the timeless nature of unresolved stories.

In the weeks that followed, the group stayed connected, sharing the lingering echoes of their Milford Manor experience. The once-ordinary business trip had become a chapter in their lives that transcended the boundaries of the mundane, a tale to be recounted and reflected upon for years to come.

Milford Manor, now free from the specters of its dark past, stood as a testament to the courage of those who dared to confront the unknown. As the office workers resumed their daily lives, they carried with them the lessons learned within the haunted halls of the historic hotel – a reminder that even in the face of the supernatural, the human spirit could prevail and find solace in the most unexpected places.

And so, the tale of the office workers and Milford Manor came to an end. The once-haunted hotel stood silent against the backdrop of New Zealand's majestic landscapes, its secrets now laid to rest. The echoes of the Pembroke family's tragic history faded into the past, leaving the travelers with memories that would forever shape their understanding of the mysterious and the supernatural.

As they resumed their lives, the office workers carried the resilience they had discovered within Milford Manor, a resilience that transcended the boundaries of the living and the dead. The routine business trip had unfolded into a journey of self-discovery, camaraderie, and the unraveling of enigmatic tales.

The memories of Milford Manor lingered, a testament to the power of confronting the unknown and the transformative impact of shared experiences. The travelers returned to their ordinary lives, forever changed by the haunting mystery that had unfolded in the heart of New Zealand.

And so, the doors of Milford Manor closed, but the echoes of its past remained, whispered through the winds that swept across Lake Wakatipu. The dark secrets and the enigma within its walls became part of the tapestry of the travelers' lives, a story to be shared, retold, and pondered upon as they continued their journey through the ever-unfolding chapters of existence.

THE PSYCHOPATH

In Ukraine, Emily, a brilliant student, carries a trouble from a scientific experiment that unleashed uncontrollable anger within her. The experiment, meant to enhance cognitive abilities, turned her into a creature of fury, complicating her new life in unfamiliar streets. Balancing her ambitious facade with inner turmoil, Emily grapples with the consequences of the experiment, making each step in her fresh start a delicate negotiation between promise and haunting shadows.

XII

THE ECHOES OF THE PAST

The decision to venture beyond the familiar confines of my homeland was a weighty one, shrouded in the mist of uncertainty. Ukraine beckoned with the allure of novel opportunities, presenting a vast canvas upon which I could artfully paint the tapestry of my fresh dreams. I am Emily, a young woman standing at the precipice of a new chapter, carrying within me a rich interplay of emotions and an undeniable yearning for a brighter tomorrow.

The process of meticulously packing my belongings was both a tangible and emotional journey. Each item carefully placed in my suitcase held not just practical significance but also embodied memories, hopes, and the haunting echoes of my mother's pleas. Her gaze, a window into both love and concern, lingered in my mind as she implored, "Emily, there's a sense of uncertainty within you. Seek a haven where the winds of change are gentler."

These words became a haunting prelude to the unknown that awaited me in this foreign land. Despite the apprehension lingering within, my resolve to explore beyond the shadows of my past drowned out the caution, propelling me into the embrace of the unfamiliar.

Upon reaching Ukraine, the streets unfolded a welcoming tapestry of cultural richness and the promise of adventure. Securing an apartment marked the initiation of a new phase in my life, and as the novelty of my surroundings unfurled, so did the intricacies of my newfound existence. Days metamorphosed into a series of discoveries as I navigated through the city—tasting local cuisine, absorbing the vibrant colors of markets, and gradually assimilating into the community.

In the midst of this odyssey of self-discovery, connections were forged with fellow companions. Among them, Tiffany—an exchange student and my dormitory roommate—stood out, her vibrant personality illuminating the path of my unfamiliar terrain. Our friendship blossomed over shared meals and explorations, with Tiffany becoming a beacon of guidance in this foreign landscape.

Over casual conversations, Tiffany divulged tales of opportunities within a scientific community that transcended the ordinary. Her narratives hinted at a unique job offer—an opportunity to become a test subject for scientific experiments. Intrigued and enticed by the promise of adventure, Tiffany handed me a number belonging to Cantch, the gatekeeper to this mysterious job opportunity.

Engaging in a conversation with Cantch unfolded over several days through messages—a virtual labyrinth of words. Our exchange became a tapestry of aspirations and the imperative need for employment. Cantch reciprocated by revealing intricate details about the job offer within the scientific community, the communication carrying an air of secrecy with hints of a clandestine meeting near a tunnel.

Despite the unconventional setting, a potent blend of curiosity and financial need led me to agree to the meeting. Some days later, near the designated tunnel, I met Cantch in person. He presented me with the job offer that would dramatically alter the trajectory of my life—an opportunity to be a test subject in a scientific experiment.

The prospect of quick earnings and the allure of new beginnings overshadowed any reservations I may have harbored. In a moment of decision, I accepted the offer, unknowingly setting in motion a series of events that would transcend the ordinary and plunge me into the depths of the unknown.

The laboratory's sterile walls, the hum of machinery, and the metallic taste of anticipation became indelible markers on the path that led me to the present. The financial remedy I initially sought transformed into a mysterious opportunity, and the experiment, yet to unfold, hinted at the Pandora's box of unforeseen consequences it held within.

Regret, a potential companion, loomed in the shadows of my future. The experiment, initially embraced for its promise of financial relief, now held the potential to reshape my destiny in ways I could not foresee. The whispers of my mother's concern, now mingling with the excitement of new opportunities, set the stage for a complex and enthralling journey through the Ukrainian landscape.

Reflecting upon that departure, the weight of my choices lingers—a poignant melody accompanying the unfolding chapters of my tumultuous existence. Ukraine, with its promise of renewal, inadvertently became the canvas where the storm within me painted its darkest hues.

In Ukraine, the whispers of my mother's concern still lingered, a haunting melody that accompanied my every step. The streets, initially painted with the promise of adventure, soon revealed the complexities of my chosen path.

As the days progressed, my existence became entangled with the enigmatic experiment that shrouded itself in shadows. Messages summoned me whenever my presence was required at the designated location. Initially, the prospect of earning nearly $20,000 per experiment seemed like a lucrative deal in the early days. However, the realization of my mistake dawned on me almost immediately. Flashbacks carried me to a pivotal moment in our humble home, where my mother's earnest pleas tried to dissuade me from the tempest I carried within.

Her words, a cautionary tale, echoed louder with each passing day. The storm within me manifested in the form of internal struggles with anger management, a consequence of the experiment I had willingly subjected myself to in pursuit of financial relief.

The experiment, born from desperation, unfolded within the recesses of my memories. A scientific endeavor promising cognitive enhancement, it turned into a Pandora's box, releasing an unbridled tempest of emotions. The sterile walls of the laboratory witnessed my transformation into a creature of uncontrollable rage, the consequences of which I grappled with daily.

As I traversed the unfamiliar streets, the initial allure of quick money that had beckoned me to be a test subject now appeared as a fool's bargain. The experiment, originally perceived as a means to escape financial hardship, had inadvertently become the catalyst for the unpredictable storm that raged within me. The internal turmoil mirrored the external chaos I had sought to leave behind, and the promise of a fresh start in Ukraine began to unravel.

Each unpredictable outburst transformed me into the antagonist in my own narrative—a symbol of the turmoil both within and around me. The echoes of my mother's pleas, initially dismissed, now reverberated louder, serving as a stark reminder of the tempest that had relentlessly followed me across borders.

The experiment metamorphosed into a haunting melody, growing more haunting with each passing day, with regret as its constant companion. The canvas of my new life, once painted with the promise of renewal, now revealed the darker hues of the storm within. The whispers of my mother's concern, entwined with my own internal struggles, set the stage for a complex and tumultuous journey through the Ukrainian landscape.

XIII

UNLEASHED FURY

The once-promising streets of Ukraine, symbolic of a new beginning, now bore witness to the zenith of my internal struggles. The echoes of my mother's concern, though seemingly distant, reverberated like a haunting refrain—a melody underscoring the intricate layers of my chosen path.

As the days seamlessly melded into weeks, the intricacies of my new life became entwined with the repercussions of a mysterious experiment. Shadows loomed larger with each unpredictable outburst, and the sterile laboratory, where my destiny underwent a profound shift, etched itself as an indelible part of my memories—an enigmatic echo of the tempest unleashed within.

The imperative to confront the scientists who orchestrated the experiment intensified. Driven by an insatiable need for answers and resolution, I embarked on a journey to untangle the mysteries of my past. The impact of the experiment on my mental state became increasingly apparent, and the weight of deciding whether to control or channel my newfound rage for the greater good bore down on my shoulders.

Amidst the unfolding chapters of my Ukrainian saga, redemption remained elusive. Whether through a sacrificial pursuit of redemption or a climactic confrontation with my inner demons, the trajectory of my story leaned tragically. The canvas of my new life, once infused with the promise of renewal, now bore the indelible marks of the choices I had made.

Regret, a relentless companion, echoed through the chambers of my soul. The experiment, conceived in the crucible of desperation, left an enduring scar on my existence. The streets of Ukraine, mere witnesses to my internal tempest, now carried the subtle shadows of my journey—shadows that stretched into the unknown, foretelling a future intricately entangled with the consequences of the storm within.

As the enigmatic experiment continued to cast its long shadows over my life, I found myself standing at the precipice of a crucial juncture—a confrontation with the architects of my altered destiny.

Fueled by an uncontrollable need for answers, I embarked on a quest to unveil the secrets concealed within the sterile walls of the laboratory. The whispers of my mother's concern, acting as a guiding force, impelled me to face the scientists who, with their experiment, had unleashed a tempest of uncontrollable rage within me.

The journey led me deep into the heart of the scientific enclave, where masked figures huddled in rooms resonating with the constant hum of machinery. The air, fraught with tension, crackled as I demanded explanations for the havoc they had wrought upon my mind. Their faces, concealed by the masks of detachment, betrayed no emotion as they recounted the unintended consequences of their experiment.

The revelation unfolded that the experiment was not an isolated incident but part of a clandestine initiative veiled in secrecy. The cognitive enhancement they sought to achieve had eluded their grasp, and inadvertently, they had transformed me into a creature of unpredictable fury. This revelation struck like a discordant chord, resonating with the dissonance within me and plunging me further into the intricate web of my own unraveling narrative.

The realization of being entangled in a larger, covert initiative left me grappling with the moral implications of my unwitting participation. The threads of secrecy woven into the experiment unraveled, revealing a tapestry of consequences that extended beyond my personal strife. The scientists, once detached and emotionless, now faced the ramifications of their pursuit—a pursuit that had inadvertently unleashed chaos upon unsuspecting test subjects like me.

The chapters of my Ukrainian saga took an unforeseen turn as I grappled with the newfound knowledge. The contours of my journey expanded, revealing the interconnectedness of my struggles with a broader narrative—one that extended beyond personal redemption to the moral quandaries of scientific ambition.

In the midst of this revelation, the whispers of my mother's concern evolved into a guiding force, urging me not just to confront the architects of my altered destiny but to confront the ethical dilemmas woven into the fabric of the scientific enclave. The sterile walls of the laboratory, once a symbol of detached curiosity, now echoed with the weight of responsibility.

As I navigated the corridors of the scientific enclave, conversations with the masked figures evolved from confrontations to a nuanced exploration of the unintended consequences of their experiments. The air, once thick with tension, now vibrated with a shared recognition of the moral complexities inherent in the pursuit of scientific progress.

My role shifted from being a mere test subject to a catalyst for introspection within the scientific community. The scientists, once veiled in secrecy, now grappled with the ethical repercussions of their actions. The revelations prompted a collective reevaluation of priorities, leading to a collaborative effort to mitigate the unintended consequences of their experiments.

The Ukrainian landscape, initially painted with the shadows of my personal tempest, now bore witness to a transformative process. The streets, once haunted by the echoes of my internal struggles, became a backdrop for an unfolding narrative of collective introspection and societal responsibility.

In the midst of this evolution, the relationship with my mother's cautionary whispers took on a new dimension. Her words, once a reminder of personal turmoil, became a guiding light in navigating the uncharted territory of ethical dilemmas. The journey, initially defined by personal redemption, now intertwined with a larger quest for ethical reckoning.

The canvas of my new life, once overshadowed by regret, now reflected the resilience and adaptability of the human spirit. The Ukrainian streets, witness to the peaks and valleys of my internal struggles, became a testament to the transformative power of confronting one's demons and, in turn, inspiring change in others.

The chapters of my Ukrainian saga continued to unfold, each page revealing the evolution of personal redemption into a collective endeavor. The sterile laboratory, once a symbol of isolated experimentation, now stood as a metaphor for the interconnectedness of individual choices with broader societal implications.

As the shadows of my personal tempest began to dissipate, a newfound sense of purpose emerged. The Ukrainian landscape, once a battleground for internal strife, now bore the footprints of a collective journey toward ethical awareness and societal responsibility. The echoes of my mother's concern, once haunting, now resonated with a sense of vindication—a testament to the transformative potential inherent in confronting the storms within and beyond.

As I delved deeper into the intricacies of the experiment's aftermath, the clash between my pursuit of control and the unpredictable forces within me intensified. The dissonance reverberated through the chapters of my tumultuous journey, weaving a complex tapestry of internal struggles and external challenges. Ukraine, once envisioned as a canvas of renewal, now bore witness to the unraveling thread of my existence.

The echoes of our confrontation lingered in the air like unresolved chords, each step on Ukraine's streets mirroring the fractures in my connections. The unintended repercussions of the experiment had morphed into a tangible force, reshaping the very essence of my being. The once-clear path to renewal now seemed shrouded in uncertainty, overshadowed by the cracks that had formed in my internal tempest.

Navigating the streets became a metaphor for traversing the broken bonds and shattered remnants of my aspirations. Each cobblestone beneath my feet marked a path laden with uncertainty, echoing the whispers of a past refusing to be silenced. The clash between my past desires for quick money and the unforeseen consequences of the experiment left me entangled in a web of regret.

The haunting shadow cast by the revelation that the experiment was part of a clandestine initiative weighed heavily on my thoughts. The scientists, concealed behind their masks of detachment, had unwittingly shaped me into a creature of unpredictable fury. The once sterile laboratory, a beacon of scientific curiosity, stood as a stark reminder of the unforeseen consequences woven into my identity.

The moral implications of their actions continued to press upon me, like an unrelenting weight on my conscience. The experiment, conceived in the crucible of desperation for financial relief, had not only altered the course of my life but had also severed the ties that connected me to the world. The quest for renewal in Ukraine now seemed like a distant dream, elusive amidst the chaos that had manifested in my internal tempest.

The broken bonds and shattered remnants of my aspirations laid bare before me as I navigated the streets. The quest for redemption surged within me, fueled by the realization that each step carried the weight of choices that had led me to this pivotal moment. The cobblestone streets stretched out, offering a path laden with uncertainty and echoes from a past that refused to be silenced.

As I continued to grapple with the aftermath of the experiment, the quest for redemption evolved into a nuanced exploration of self-discovery. The clash between my pursuit of control and the unpredictable forces within me became a crucible for transformation. Ukraine, once a canvas marred by the storm within, now held the potential for a new narrative—one defined by resilience and the ability to confront the shadows of the past.

The echoes of our confrontation faded into the background, replaced by the persistent rhythm of my footsteps on Ukraine's streets. Each stride became a testament to the strength forged in the crucible of internal and external challenges. The unintended repercussions of the experiment, while casting a long shadow, also paved the way for a journey of introspection and eventual renewal.

The secrets unveiled in the sterile laboratory, once a haunting reminder, now became stepping stones on the path to revelation and redemption. The once-fractured connections within me began to mend, and the broken bonds found the possibility of being rewoven into a tapestry of resilience. The cobblestone streets, once marked by uncertainty, now bore witness to the evolving narrative of self-discovery and the pursuit of a renewed existence.

Ukraine, with its complex landscape and the echoes of my tumultuous journey, transformed into a metaphorical crucible—a place where the storm within met the resilience of the human spirit. The unraveling thread of my existence now held the promise of being rewoven into a tapestry enriched by the colors of introspection, redemption, and the enduring quest for renewal.

XIV

THE WHISPER OF REDEMPTION

The Ukrainian streets, once a symbol of promise, now cradled the weight of my choices as I embarked on the next leg of my journey. The echoes of the confrontation with the scientists still resonated, urging me to seek redemption from the shadows cast by the experiment.

As the night fell, casting shadows dancing with the faint glow of streetlights, I felt compelled to explore the heart of Ukraine's mysteries. The city's rhythm, a gentle hum, seemed to align with the beats of my own quest—an exploration of understanding, redemption, and the hope for a new beginning.

The layers of the city unfolded like the pages of a story, revealing tales written into its buildings, culture, and the spirit of its people. The echoes of my footsteps harmonized with the sounds of laughter, music, and the distant hum of life unfolding in the urban fabric.

The journey became a dance between the external world and my inner quest. Every encounter, every shared moment with newfound friends, added another stroke to the evolving canvas of my redemption. The city, once unfamiliar, now felt like a living entity woven into the story of my transformation.

The echoes of the experiment, though still present, began to lose their grip as I delved deeper into Ukraine. The mystery of the scientists and their secret initiative became a subplot in the larger drama of self-discovery and resilience.

In the company of those who became my confidants, the shadows of my past seemed to fade. The winding streets, once confusing, now guided me towards clarity. The Ukrainian nights became a backdrop for conversations unraveling the complexities of our shared journeys and the common thread of redemption.

As the stars lit up the night sky, I stood on the verge of a revelation. The culmination of my journey approached, promising either a triumphant emergence from the shadows or a descent into the unknown. The Ukrainian streets, witnesses to my inner struggles, seemed to hold their breath in anticipation.

The labyrinth had become a tapestry of experiences, interwoven with the rich fabric of Ukrainian life. The climax awaited, a moment where the echoes of the experiment would either dissipate or reverberate into eternity. In the heart of Ukraine, amidst the vibrant symphony of life, I prepared for the final act of my redemption saga.

Amidst the rhythmic sounds of the city, I sought out Cantch, the mysterious figure linked to the experiment that had disrupted my life. Attempts to confront him with questions proved fruitless, as he remained elusive, providing no answers to the queries that echoed through my mind.

The Ukrainian nights, once filled with the promise of renewal, now carried the weight of unresolved mysteries. Cantch, a shadowy presence in the narrative of my redemption, seemed to embody the enigma that continued to elude me. The stars overhead witnessed my persistent quest for answers, their silent gleam reflecting the uncertainty in the Ukrainian air.

As my journey reached its zenith, the Ukrainian streets became a stage for the final act—a confrontation that would either reveal the shadows or plunge me into the unknown. The echoes of my footsteps, accompanied by the pulse of the city, resonated with determination, for I was poised to unravel the last strands of the enigmatic tapestry that bound me to Cantch and the haunting experiment.

The streets, once silent witnesses to my struggles, now stood as the arena where destiny awaited its final reckoning. In the labyrinth of emotions, I navigated towards Cantch, the last piece of the puzzle that could decipher the cryptic language of the experiment. The night air carried a sense of urgency as I approached the rendezvous point—a quiet alley bathed in the soft glow of a single lamppost.

Cantch emerged from the shadows, his features obscured in the dim light. The air crackled with tension as I confronted him, demanding answers that had eluded me for far too long. But Cantch, ever enigmatic, responded with a cryptic smile, offering no solace to the storm within me.

The exchange unfolded like a carefully choreographed dance of words, each step leading me deeper into the labyrinth of uncertainty. Cantch remained a master of evasion, skillfully diverting my inquiries with vague explanations and elusive rhetoric.

In the midst of our verbal sparring, the city seemed to hold its breath, as if aware of the gravity of the encounter. The Ukrainian streets, witnesses to my odyssey, stood silent, awaiting the revelation that hung in the balance.

As the conversation with Cantch reached an impasse, a realization dawned upon me—the answers I sought might remain forever elusive. The shadows of the experiment, once menacing, now seemed to retreat into the background, leaving me standing alone in the Ukrainian night.

With a sense of acceptance, I turned away from Cantch, allowing the weight of unanswered questions to dissipate into the nocturnal air. The labyrinth, though still fraught with uncertainties, no longer seemed insurmountable. The Ukrainian streets, once shrouded in mystery, now beckoned me towards a new chapter—one where redemption would be defined not by answers, but by the resilience to forge ahead.

The echoes of the confrontation lingered, yet a newfound determination replaced the lingering shadows. The Ukrainian streets, once a symbol of confusion, now paved the way for the next chapter of my journey—an unwritten story of self-discovery and the pursuit of a brighter tomorrow.

XV

THE FINAL REVELATION

The streets of Ukraine bore witness to a confession that resonated beyond the shadows of my past. Fueled by the urgent need for redemption, I decided to unburden the tempest within my soul to those who could bring about justice.

With determination in my steps, I sought out the authorities, the keepers of law and order. The labyrinth of my internal struggles now mirrored the official intricacies I faced. The vibrant hues of the country seemed to fade as I navigated through the corridors of power, each step echoing with the weight of my revelation.

In a dimly lit room, I poured out the details of the experiment, the consequences, and the moral implications to those who held the keys to justice. The confession became a cathartic release, a narrative woven with threads of truth, vulnerability, and the unrelenting pursuit of redemption.

The decision to approach the government office was not an easy one. As each day passed, the experiment's impact manifested in an alarming transformation within me. The once-subtle rage had grown into a force that threatened to engulf my very essence. It was a realization that compelled me to confront my mistakes and seek redemption for the chaos I had unwittingly become.

As I made my way through the bureaucratic maze, the weight of my revelation hung heavy in the air. Andrei, the dedicated investigator who had become an ally in the pursuit of justice, accompanied me. The streets outside, once witnesses to my internal turmoil, seemed to hold their breath as I stepped into the government office to confess my involvement in the experiment.

The authorities, stirred by the gravity of my revelation, took swift action. Investigations were launched, and the scientists responsible for the experiment were brought to justice. The streets, though silent witnesses, seemed to resonate with the collective sigh of a system confronting its own shadows.

In the aftermath, Andrei and I continued our collaborative efforts. As we worked together to unravel the remaining mysteries, the bond between us strengthened. The shared pursuit of justice evolved into a partnership forged in the crucible of redemption.

Amidst the complexities of our mission, I discovered a different kind of warmth in Andrei's presence. The streets, now witnesses to our shared pursuit of justice, seemed to bridge the gap between duty and an unforeseen connection.

As the investigation unfolded, a subtle shift occurred. The tempest within me, once a force of uncontrollable rage, found solace in Andrei's company. Our shared commitment to justice evolved into a shared understanding, and, against all odds, the tendrils of affection unfurled.

The journey had taken an unexpected turn—a turn that led not only to justice but also to the blossoming of an unforeseen connection. The Ukrainian streets, once shrouded in shadows, now bore witness to the emergence of a new chapter—a chapter where redemption and the unexpected dance harmoniously.

Amidst the unfolding investigation, the streets of Ukraine became the silent observers of justice taking its course. The scientists faced the consequences of their actions, and the intricate web of my internal struggles began to untangle, offering a semblance of closure.

In the shared pursuit of justice, a bond flourished between the dedicated Andrei and me. Together, we navigated the complexities of the aftermath, forging a connection that surpassed the boundaries of duty. The streets, once witnesses to my internal turmoil, now held the echoes of our shared journey.

As time passed, a subtle transformation occurred. The investigator, initially a symbol of justice, evolved into a comforting presence. His company became a refuge for the tempest within me, blurring the lines between duty and personal connection.

The unexpected affection that sprouted amid the shadows of our mission caught us both off guard. The streets, witnesses to both justice and the complexities of emotions, portrayed the evolving narrative of our relationship. The complexity of our roles, the shadows of the experiments, and the unexpected twists of affection painted a tapestry that added depth to our story.

In the heart of Ukraine, against the backdrop of a city that had seen both turmoil and redemption, our connection grew stronger. The streets, bearing the weight of my past, seemed to guide us towards a path where affection and redemption coexisted—an unexpected union that defied the odds and added a new layer to the evolving story of my journey.

As the tapestry of my journey continued to weave, fate took an unexpected turn. The shadows that once haunted me, the echoes of my tempest, led to an inevitable destination—an end that mirrored the chapters of my life. The authorities asserted that it was for my safety and the well-being of those around me. They claimed that the experiment had induced changes in my DNA, making me uniquely adaptable to a potentially dangerous rage that could escalate if I continued to live. Placing a pen and paper in front of me, they presented a document stating that I had chosen to sacrifice myself for everyone's safety. With no apparent alternative, given the newfound power that could pose a global threat, I tearfully signed the document, left with no other choice.

In the quiet solitude of a dimly lit room, I put pen to paper for the last time. The weight of my experiences, the whispers of affection, and the journey towards redemption found their final refuge on the pages of a diary. The streets, no longer witnesses to my footsteps, held the echoes of a story that had reached its conclusion.

As the ink dried, the inevitable descended. The tempest within me, once a force of uncontrollable rage, now found its stillness. The echoes of my existence, the shadows that danced through the labyrinth of my life, faded into the silence of an ending. Then for the last time, I opened my pendant to take a look at my mother's picture and kissed her goodbye.

In the aftermath, Andrei, the one who had become an unexpected anchor in my life, discovered the diary. The streets, trodden by the weight of my past, whispered their secrets to him. With a mixture of curiosity and reverence, he read through the pages that chronicled the complexities of my journey.

The diary became a portal to my inner world, a testament to the battles fought and the shadows confronted. As he delved into the intimate revelations, the investigator discovered the echoes of affection, the challenges faced, and the ultimate sacrifice that marked the closing chapter of my story.

In the quiet room, the investigator's gaze lifted from the final page. The cobblestone streets outside, bathed in the muted glow of streetlights, seemed to hold their breath. The echoes of my existence lingered in the stillness, a testament to a life that had traversed the tumultuous terrain of redemption and sacrifice.

As the investigator, Andrei closed the diary, a profound understanding settled within him. The streets, once witnesses to my struggles, now cradled the legacy of a journey that transcended the boundaries of time. The echoes, now carried in the heart of the investigator, became a silent testament to a story that had left its indelible mark on the Ukrainian streets and the heart of Andrei, who had come to understand, cherish, and mourn the complexity of my life.

THE SHADOWS WE CONFRONT

Maya, Raj, and Anjali join forces to expose a cult led by Vikram. Through infiltration, intelligence, and resilience, they dismantle the cult's grip, revealing Vikram's vulnerabilities. The story explores unity, friendship, and the triumph of truth over darkness."

XVI

UNVEILING THE CULT

The neon lights of the city flickered outside Maya's apartment window, casting a vibrant glow on the cityscape. It was well past midnight, and Maya sat hunched over her cluttered desk, surrounded by a web of newspaper clippings and hastily written notes. The room echoed with the low hum of the city, a background melody to the unfolding mystery before her.

Raj, her trusted friend and colleague, shuffled in from the kitchen with a steaming cup of coffee. "What's got you burning the midnight oil, Maya?"

Maya looked up, her eyes filled with shock. "Raj, I've got something big. An anonymous tip about a series of murders connected to a cult. A cult, Raj! This could be a part of a neferious plan or sinster plot!"

Raj's eyebrows shot up in surprise. "A cult? You sure about this, Maya?"

Maya nodded, waving a mysterious letter in front of him. "This arrived earlier. Cryptic, but it's pointing to something sinister. We need to dig deeper."

As Raj studied the letter, Maya began connecting the dots on a corkboard, creating a chaotic yet strangely organized web of information. The room buzzed with energy, a palpable sense of urgency that fueled their shared passion for uncovering the truth.

"Anjali might have something for us," Maya mused, referring to her sister, who worked as a nurse at a local hospital. "She's overheard things—whispers among cult members seeking medical attention. We could leverage that information."

Raj nodded, his analytical mind already racing. "Smart move. Let's see what Anjali can unearth for us."

Cut to Maya's cozy apartment, where Anjali sat across from her sister, worry etched across her face. "Maya, I've heard the rumors at the hospital. This investigation...it's dangerous. You have to be careful."

Maya offered a reassuring smile. "Anjali, I've got Raj with me. We're a team, and we'll expose this cult together. Trust me."

Anjali sighed, knowing she couldn't dissuade Maya from her mission. "Just promise me you'll watch your back and keep Raj close. You two make a formidable team."

Back at their makeshift office, Raj and Maya delved into the research, their friendship and camaraderie evident in the way they seamlessly bounced ideas off each other. The room echoed with the clicking of keyboards and the occasional laughter, a testament to the bond they shared.

"You have a knack for stumbling upon the weirdest stories, Maya," Raj remarked, a playful smirk on his face.

Maya chuckled, "And you have a way of turning chaos into coherence. We make a great team, Raj."

As the night wore on, the trio's energy increased. Anjali, though not physically present, played a crucial role in the investigation. Her information from the hospital opened doors to the cult's activities, providing Maya and Raj with valuable leads.

"You know," Raj said, glancing at Maya with a genuine smile, "I wouldn't want to unravel this mystery with anyone else by my side."

Maya returned the sentiment, "Likewise, Raj. We're in this together."

Little did they know that the investigation was about to take a perilous turn, and the cult's ominous leader, had already set his sights on Maya. As they delved deeper into the shadows, the friendship between Maya, Raj, and Anjali would be put to the ultimate test in a deadly game of cat and mouse. The city, with its secrets and shadows, held a darkness they were only just beginning to comprehend.

XVII

UNPREDICTABLE MOVE

Maya, Raj, and Anjali continued their pursuit of the cult's secrets, with Maya now inside Vikram's mansion. Anjali, increasingly worried for her sister's safety, couldn't stay on the sidelines any longer.

From their base, Anjali whispered through the earpiece, "Maya, please be careful. I've got a bad feeling about this."

Maya reassured her, "I'll be fine, Anjali. Just keep watch from there."

Unable to shake her concern, Anjali decided to dig deeper. Through her position at the hospital, she uncovered a crucial piece of information—some cult members had sought medical attention for mysterious illnesses related to Vikram's experiments.

Anjali reached out to Maya with this insight, advising, "Maya, some cult members have medical issues tied to Vikram's experiments. Use this to your advantage."

Grateful for Anjali's help, Maya adjusted her approach, subtly sowing doubt among the cult members about Vikram's true intentions.

Unbeknownst to Maya, Vikram became suspicious. Anjali sensed the danger and urgently warned, "Maya, be cautious. Vikram's onto something."

Vikram's henchmen, tracing Anjali's activities, confronted her at the hospital. Faced with the threat, Anjali stood her ground, refusing to be silenced. She triggered an alarm, drawing attention to the danger.

Raj, monitoring from their base, picked up on the signal. Realizing the threat to Anjali, Maya urgently messaged, "Anjali, get out of there now!"

With Raj's guidance, Anjali managed to escape. Though shaken, she remained determined to support Maya in exposing the cult's secrets.

The trio now faced heightened danger, their quest for truth intensifying as they navigated the shadows of the cult's sinister machinations.

Maya's investigation took a crucial turn when her editor-in-chief, Ravi, assigned her the task of delving into the mysterious cult. Ravi, a seasoned journalist and a friend to Maya, believed in her skills but cautioned her against unnecessary risks.

One evening, as Maya continued her research, Ravi called her into his office. "Maya, I've got something for you. An anonymous source mentioned a connection between the cult and some influential figures in the city. Be careful, this could lead to something big."

Maya, fueled by Ravi's support, intensified her efforts. As she connected the dots on her corkboard, Ravi occasionally provided insights from his extensive network of contacts, guiding her through the labyrinth of secrets.

Ravi often reminded her, "Maya, trust your instincts, but never underestimate the dangers you might face. We need the truth, but your safety comes first."

Meanwhile, Vikram's wife, Priya, remained a haunting presence in his life. The revelations of her loyalty to Vikram and her role in his illegal experiments were like a shadow over Maya's investigation. Priya's connection to Maya's father, the man who exposed Vikram's crimes, added another layer of complexity.

Maya, driven by the quest for truth and justice, knew she had to confront Vikram's dark past, uncover Priya's secrets, and expose the cult's influence on the city.

XVIII

UNCOVERING WEAKNESS

The night hung heavy with tension as Maya, fueled by Anjali's sacrifice, pressed on in her mission within Vikram's mansion. With Anjali's crucial information about the cult members' medical history, Maya strategized to exploit the growing uncertainty among the followers.

As Maya delved deeper into the mansion's secret chambers, she overheard conversations that hinted at Vikram's weakness. His obsession with maintaining an appearance of supernatural power was driven by a rare genetic disorder causing rapid aging and loss of vitality. This revelation was the key to dismantling the charismatic facade Vikram had carefully built.

Maya, now armed with this powerful knowledge, reached out to Raj through their secure communication channel. "Raj, I've found something big. Vikram's weakness is a genetic disorder. It's what's driving his pursuit of supernatural power."

Raj, processing the information, replied, "That's a game-changer, Maya. Exploit it, but be careful. We don't know how he'll react."

Maya, driven by a newfound determination, subtly introduced the idea of vulnerability into her conversations with cult members. Seeds of doubt took root, and whispers of Vikram's mortality spread among the followers.

Vikram, unaware of Maya's discoveries, intensified his efforts to quell dissent within the cult. As Maya navigated the dangerous dance of deception, she witnessed a shift in the cult's dynamics. The once unwavering loyalty of Vikram's followers began to waver, and skepticism cast a shadow over his grand plans.

Raj, monitoring from their base, observed the ripple effect of Maya's actions. "You're doing great, Maya. Keep up the pressure."

Maya, now on a razor's edge between exposure and triumph, formulated a plan to confront Vikram directly. She needed to exploit his weakness and expose his vulnerability to the very followers who worshipped him.

In a carefully orchestrated confrontation, Maya challenged Vikram's supposed invincibility. Armed with the knowledge of his genetic disorder, she shattered the illusion he had crafted, revealing the very mortal man behind the charismatic leader.

Vikram, faced with the revelation of his weakness, recoiled in shock and anger. The once loyal cult members, now disillusioned, questioned their allegiance. Maya seized the moment, addressing the followers, "Vikram's pursuit of power is driven by fear. He's not the all-powerful leader you believe him to be."

As doubt spread like wildfire among the cult members, Vikram's influence crumbled. Maya, with Raj's guidance, led a contingent of followers who were disillusioned by the truth. Together, they made a daring escape from the mansion, leaving Vikram isolated in the ruins of his once grand illusion.

The city's night whispered of victory, but Maya knew the battle was far from over. Vikram, fueled by rage and desperation, would not rest until he retaliated. The trio, now more united than ever, prepared for the final showdown that would determine the fate of the cult and the safety of those entangled in its dark web.

Maya's investigation reached a critical juncture, with Ravi providing valuable leads and guidance. The trio, now including Ravi in their virtual meetings, strategized their next moves.

Ravi suggested, "Maya, focus on Priya's background. It might be the key to understanding Vikram's motives and vulnerabilities."

Anjali, drawing on her medical insights, dug deeper into Priya's history, uncovering her scientific contributions and her involvement in Vikram's experiments. The revelation that Priya was once a scientist who aided Vikram fueled Maya's determination.

As they continued their investigation, Ravi cautioned, "Maya, tread carefully. Priya's past is intertwined with Vikram's, and it might hold the key to unraveling the cult's dark secrets."

Maya, armed with newfound information about Priya's role, confronted Vikram's followers, sowing seeds of doubt about their leader's true intentions. Ravi's journalistic expertise guided Maya in crafting a compelling narrative to expose the cult's activities.

Simultaneously, Anjali uncovered Priya's tragic end at the hands of Maya's father. This revelation added an emotional layer to the already complex web of relationships within the cult.

XIX

THE VICORTIOUS ESCAPE

After Maya spilled the truth about Vikram's weaknesses, his control over the cult started falling apart. Confused followers questioned their loyalty. Maya, Raj, and the group found a safe spot to plan their next steps.

Raj warned, "Maya, Vikram won't give up easily. We need solid evidence against him."

Working together, they gathered proof to expose the cult's activities. Anjali, recovered from her previous troubles, joined the team.

As they prepared to share their findings, Vikram, feeling desperate, struck back. The remaining loyal cult members backed him, turning the situation into a dangerous game. It became a fight between Maya's group and Vikram's followers.

In a tense moment, Vikram confronted Maya. "You won't ruin everything I've built!" he shouted.

But Maya, with her team by her side, stood strong. "Your fear tactics end now. We won't let you hurt anyone else."

A fierce battle erupted, with Maya, Raj, and Anjali fighting against the cult members. In the chaos, Maya faced Vikram in a final showdown.

Their clash was intense. Maya, using Vikram's own vulnerability against him, exposed his weaknesses to his followers. As the truth sank in, Vikram's control crumbled.

Authorities, tipped off by Maya's evidence, arrived to restore order. Vikram, caught and defeated, tried to escape but was captured.

Maya, Raj, and Anjali emerged victorious, dismantling the cult's influence. The city, once under a dark shadow, began healing.

Reflecting on their journey, the trio knew the fight against darkness continued. United by trust, they faced the challenges ahead, ensuring the city stayed a place of light and strength.

Vikram caught, cult gone, Maya, Raj, and Anjali took a moment to breathe. The city, once in cult shadows, now bathed in truth and justice.

As cops handled things, the trio sat down to think. Anjali, glad Maya was okay, said, "You did it, Maya. Brought down the darkness."

Maya smiled, "We did it together. Faced it head-on and got stronger."

Raj, the realist, added, "But we stay watchful. Other shadows might linger."

United, they kept working together. Forming a tight team, they vowed to uncover any threats to the city.

Walking the quiet streets, they saw scars but also signs of hope. The city, once scared, was ready for a new beginning.

Maya, Raj, and Anjali joined local groups, helping those hurt by the cult. They became local heroes, fighting against injustice.

Months passed, and the city changed. Safer and more united, thanks to Maya, Raj, and Anjali.

Looking at the skyline, Maya said, "We faced the dark, but brought light back. Together, we're strong."

Raj agreed, "And we'll stay strong. Together, the city stays tough."

Anjali, watching the sun go down, added, "This is a new start for us and the city. We'll face anything that comes our way."

With the past shadows gone, Maya, Raj, and Anjali embraced a new beginning. The city, once in a cult's grip, now stood strong, showing that friendship, unity, and a search for truth can beat any darkness.

As Maya, Raj, and Anjali closed in on the truth, Ravi's mentorship proved invaluable. He urged Maya to remain vigilant and maintain her journalistic integrity in the face of increasing danger.

Ravi shared, "Maya, you're close to exposing the cult. But remember, truth can be a double-edged sword. Stay focused, and don't let emotions cloud your judgment."

Anjali, still haunted by her own encounter with danger, echoed Ravi's sentiment, "Maya, be cautious. The cult is unraveling, but Vikram won't go down without a fight."

In a pivotal moment, Ravi uncovered a hidden connection between Vikram and some powerful individuals in the city. He urged Maya to expose this link, knowing it could bring the cult's reign of terror to an end.

Maya, with unwavering determination, confronted Vikram's wife, Priya's tragic past, and the influential figures linked to the cult. Ravi's guidance and Anjali's medical insights converged, creating a powerful narrative that would expose Vikram's web of deceit.

As they prepared to publish their findings, Ravi emphasized, "Maya, this is your moment. The city needs to know the truth. But remember, the aftermath might be as challenging as the investigation itself."

Little did they know that the final confrontation with Vikram awaited them, and the revelation of his darkest secrets would bring the cult to its knees.

About The Author

At the tender age of 14, Deetya Agarwal Pareek emerges as a prodigious talent, casting a remarkable presence in the literary realm. A fervent devotee of the English language, Deetya has risen to prominence for her spellbinding novels, which have found a home on various platforms. Her journey as an author embarked upon its course during her early years, nurtured by the steadfast encouragement of her parents, who recognized and fostered her innate storytelling gift.

Deetya's writing stands as a testament not only to her innate talent but also to her unwavering dedication to the craft. Her novels, born out of a genuine love for literature, have resonated with readers spanning geographical boundaries. With a portfolio that continues to burgeon and a knack for weaving captivating narratives, Deetya Agarwal Pareek is poised to etch an enduring imprint on the literary panorama.

Embark on a journey through the enthralling worlds she meticulously crafts, and brace yourself to be captivated by the literary prowess of this young and promising author.

www.ingramcontent.com/pod-product-compliance
Lightning Source LLC
LaVergne TN
LVHW041114150826
845673LV00007B/2042

* 9 7 9 8 8 9 2 7 7 0 2 0 0 *